"Alexis, what are you thinking?"

Jace asked softly.

"I'm thinking about the kind of man you are," she replied.

Surprise flickered in his eyes. "What kind of man am I?"

"I...I think you're hard. And honest."

"I hope so. Anything else?"

She swallowed. "You like your life here and would never want to leave."

His eyes narrowed thoughtfully. "That's right. My life is here."

She had no idea where these thoughts and questions were coming from, but she went on. "Did you like being alone all the time? Because I know what it's like to live in a big place and to be lonely...."

"Do you, Alexis? I'm sorry." He raised his hand to touch her cheek. He ran his finger along her velvety skin. "Being lonely is hell. Have you been lonely since you came to Sleepy River?"

She looked into his steady dark eyes. "Not recently..."

Dear Reader,

Although the anniversary is over, Silhouette Romance is still celebrating our coming of age—we'll soon be twenty-one! Be sure to join us each and every month for six emotional stories about the romantic journey from first time to forever.

And this month we've got a special Valentine's treat for you! Three stories deal with the special holiday for true lovers. Karen Rose Smith gives us a man who asks an old friend to *Be My Bride?* Teresa Southwick's latest title, *Secret Ingredient: Love,* brings back the delightful Marchetti family. And Carla Cassidy's *Just One Kiss* shows how a confirmed bachelor is brought to his knees by a special woman.

Amusing, emotional and oh-so-captivating Carolyn Zane is at it again! Her latest BRUBAKER BRIDES story, *Tex's Exasperating Heiress,* features a determined groom, a captivating heiress and the pig that brought them together. And popular author Arlene James tells of *The Mesmerizing Mr. Carlyle,* part of our AN OLDER MAN thematic miniseries. Readers will love the overwhelming attraction between this couple! Finally, *The Runaway Princess* marks Patricia Forsythe's debut in the Romance line. But Patricia is no stranger to love stories, having written many as Patricia Knoll!

Next month, look for appealing stories by Raye Morgan, Susan Meier, Valerie Parv and other exciting authors. And be sure to return in March for a new installment of the popular ROYALLY WED tales!

Happy reading!

Mary-Theresa Hussey

Mary-Theresa Hussey
Senior Editor

Please address questions and book requests to:
Silhouette Reader Service
U.S.: 3010 Walden Ave., P.O. Box 1325, Buffalo, NY 14269
Canadian: P.O. Box 609, Fort Erie, Ont. L2A 5X3

The Runaway Princess

PATRICIA FORSYTHE

SILHOUETTE *Romance*

Published by Silhouette Books

America's Publisher of Contemporary Romance

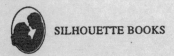

SILHOUETTE BOOKS

ISBN 0-373-19497-8

THE RUNAWAY PRINCESS

Printed In U.S.A.

PATRICIA FORSYTHE

admits that she's a lifelong daydreamer who has always enjoyed spinning stories in her head. She grew up in a copper mining town in Arizona, which was a true adventure because of the interesting characters who inhabited the place. During the years when she was going to college, earning her degree, teaching school, marrying and raising four children, those characters were in her mind. She wanted to put them in a book, but it wasn't until she discovered romance novels with their emotional content and satisfying resolutions that she found a home for those characters.

Patricia still lives in Arizona with her family and pets and continues to spin stories about interesting places and compelling characters.

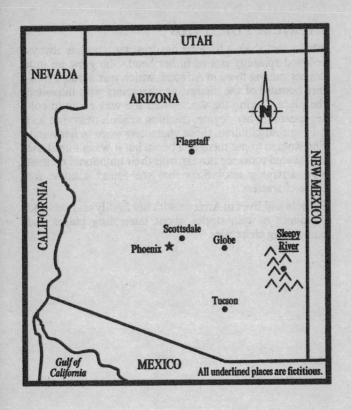

UTAH

NEVADA

ARIZONA

CALIFORNIA

NEW MEXICO

Flagstaff •

Scottsdale •

Globe •

Sleepy
River

Phoenix ★

Tucson •

Gulf of
California

MEXICO

All underlined places are fictitious.

Chapter One

Her Most Serene Royal Highness Princess Alexis Mary Charlotte of the House of Chastain and the principality of Inbourg ran out of pavement and hope at exactly the same moment.

Dumbfounded, she stared over the hood of the compact car. Where had the road gone? She had been following this dratted ribbon of asphalt through Arizona's White Mountains for hours now. It seemed like days. She'd seen nothing but trees, though she wouldn't have been surprised to come upon the last remains of a hapless traveler propped against the base of a pine tree, his bony fingers holding a sign reading Abandon All Hope.

She sighed, leaned forward over the steering wheel and peered into the darkness.

Even after she had left the highway and turned off onto this side road, everything had seemed all right.

She'd been sure that all she had to do was continue following it. Things would be fine once she reached Sleepy River. She'd been repeating it like a mantra since early that morning.

However, a few minutes ago, clouds had drifted in to cover the moon and these woods were desperately dark without its glow. This section of tall, dark pines was hardly ablaze with streetlights.

Squinting into the night, she tried to see something; a road sign, a blazed trail, a friendly native, *anything* around her besides trees, trees, and more trees.

She had long since left Morenci, the last town, far behind and she knew she couldn't turn back. Wherever she was, she knew she was closer to Sleepy River than she was to Morenci, so she might as well keep going. She gripped the steering wheel and lifted herself up to gaze forlornly over the hood. She would keep going as soon as she figured out what had become of the road.

She knew she had taken exactly the right turns every step of the way as she followed the Coronado Trail, which had supposedly been scouted out by the Spanish conquistadors four hundred years ago.

"Too bad I don't have one of them along to help me now," she muttered in annoyance. A glance at the dashboard clock told her it was after eleven o'clock. The efficient little car, borrowed from her friend Rachel Burrows, was easy to drive, but every tense and aching muscle in her body told her it was time to quit.

But how could she? Somehow she'd managed to get herself lost—a rarity for her. She would have called for help if her cell phone hadn't died on her.

Besides which, she had a map and precise directions, and she was excellent at following both. Until a few days ago, her entire life had been a perfect model of direction-following.

In spite of that, she'd done something wrong because the paved road had petered out into nothingness leaving only a dirt track for her to follow.

"Oh blast and bother," she groused.

With a discouraged sigh, she leaned her head against the steering wheel and closed her eyes. This had been the most impossibly longest day of her life and it was far from over.

Exhaustion nearly swamped her as she tried to recall exactly how all this had happened. Oh, yes. She'd been pursuing her dream; a dream of independence, self-reliance, having a career instead of being a glorified baby-sitter for her nephew. A dream of being her own person instead of the last of the three daughters of Prince Michael of Inbourg whose occupation seemed to be, as one tabloid so gracelessly put it, "Squandering the money of the citizens of Inbourg with marathon sessions of power shopping."

Never mind that her sisters, Anya and Deirdre, had been photographed buying supplies for the disaster relief society they co-chaired. Tabloid reporters didn't care about the truth, only about publishing the flashiest headlines. What would they think if they knew that Princess Alexis had taken a long-term substitute teaching job in a one-room schoolhouse in the mountains of Arizona? It didn't matter what the truth actually was. Their assignment would be to put the most negative possible spin on it.

It would be bad if the tabloids discovered that she had come to the States on the pretense of spending several weeks pampering herself at a health spa. It would be disastrous if they learned she had installed Esther Wanfray, her lady-in-waiting, there in her place.

Oh, why was she thinking about that now? Alexis looked about in quiet desperation. She had to turn around, go back, and figure out where she'd gone wrong. Carefully, she put the car in reverse and started to back up.

A sickening thud and then a splintering of wood told her she'd hit something.

"What on earth...?" Quickly, she threw the car into drive and lurched forward. This time a jarring scrape on the front right fender split the air.

"Oh, no." Horrified, Alexis stared straight ahead for an instant trying to think what to do next. Get out and take a look was the only thing that occurred to her.

She reached across the seat and scrambled in the glove compartment for the flashlight only to find to her astonishment that there wasn't one.

Suddenly furious, she sputtered as she threw open the car door and hopped out, "Oh, Rachel," she wailed. "Why don't you carry a flashlight in your car?" She stood peering into the darkness beyond the beam of the headlights for a moment, then remembered a small book of matches she'd picked up somewhere. She didn't know how much good they would be, but a little light was better than nothing.

She took the matches from her purse, struck one

carefully, and turned toward the back of the car to
see what she had hit. The wind immediately blew out
the match.

"Drat." She struck another match and tried again.
It blew out before she'd taken two steps, as did
matches number three, four and five.

Frustrated, she glanced back into the car and spied
the magazine she'd bought before boarding the plane
to Phoenix. With a glad cry, she picked it up, tore out
several pages and wrapped them into a roll. She then
lit the end and had a crude but effective torch. Holding it carefully, she moved to the rear of the vehicle
where she saw a splintered pole lying on the ground
and on the end of it, tilting crazily skyward, was a
mailbox.

"McTaggart," she read, and then read it again.
"McTaggart!" Astounded and relieved, her voice
rose an octave. "I'm in the right place." Whirling
around, she held the torch up and tried to peer farther
into the darkness. "But where's the house?"

McTaggart was the name of the school board president. She was to pick up the key to her own cottage
and to the schoolhouse from him. Now all she had to
do was figure out where the house was.

She wasn't lost, after all, she thought, elated. She
had ended up exactly where she was supposed to be.
She had reached Sleepy River community and, as
she'd been promising herself all day, everything was
going to be just fine.

Hurrying back to the front of the car, she looked
for the house, but could see nothing and finally concluded it was farther down this dirt road. Hope and

confidence surged. With the help of her trusty torch, she could find it, though she moved her hand farther down toward the end of the burning papers, and prayed the flame would last until she found the house.

In a rush, Alexis reached in and took her shoulder bag from the car, paused to lock the doors, then began moving forward cautiously. She paused to see what she'd scraped the car against when she'd pulled forward.

It was a vine-covered wall. If the moon had been out, she probably would have seen it as well as the mailbox. The damage to the car didn't appear to be too bad.

As she straightened, she heard the crunch of gravel behind her, and then a deep male voice saying, "What the devil...?"

With a start of surprise, Alexis whirled. The sudden movement fanned the flare of the torch, sending a speck of burning paper flying down to scorch her hand. With a cry, she dropped the torch into the grass beside the wall.

Immediately, the dry grass burst into flames.

"Hey," the man yelled. In the flare of light, she saw only shadows and had the impression of a large body flying past as he leaped forward to stamp out the flames. "What do you think you're doing?"

"I'm sorry," she stammered, dropping her purse beside the car and jumping onto the flames. She stomped for all she was worth but the fire was moving faster than she was. "I...I didn't see..."

Fire licked hungrily at the tinder-dry weeds and

grass. Within seconds, the flames were moving too rapidly for the two of them to handle.

"Run to the house," the man ordered. "There's a triangle on the front porch. Ring it and yell 'Fire.'"

"Yes, all right." She started to scurry away, but then stumbled around and threw out her hands desperately. "Where's the house?"

"*Where's the house?*" he repeated, astounded. "Over there where the porch light is."

Frantically, Alexis glanced around to see that, sure enough, not one hundred feet away stood a two-story ranch house with a porch light sending out a bright glow.

"How did that get there?" she gasped.

"It's been there for seventy years!"

Alexis didn't waste any more time. She dashed for the steps leading to the porch. At one end was a set of heavy redwood lawn furniture and at the other was an old-fashioned iron triangle of the type farm women had once used to call the family to supper. It hung suspended from a ceiling beam. An eight-inch rod swung from a leather loop which was threaded onto the open side of the triangle.

Shrieking, "Fire, fire, fire!" Alexis grabbed the rod and began beating the triangle until the sound rang out to who knew where.

Behind her in the house, she could hear shouts and the thumping of feet as lights were switched on. Having given the alarm, she abandoned the triangle and looked around for anything that could be used to fight the fire. She knew there was no use in trying to find a garden hose or bucket because that would waste a great deal of time. She spied a blanket folded up on a chair, snatched it up, and ran, full tilt back to the fire.

"Here," she gulped, thrusting it at the man who was fighting the blaze. He took it without a word and began beating out the flames while she continued to pound at them with her feet. A minute later, two more men joined them, dragging a long garden hose. They turned it on and within seconds, the flames were doused.

Shakily thankful, Alexis slumped against the front of the car and put her trembling hands in front of her face. A minute. She only needed a minute to compose herself.

"Hey, miss, are you all right?" one of the men asked. It wasn't the voice of the first one who'd startled her into dropping the torch.

She glanced up. Suddenly, the clouds parted, the moon shone down with a dim glow, and Alexis could see three men facing her. All of them were wearing hastily donned shirts, boots and jeans. The tallest of the three approached her furiously.

"Who are you and why are you trying to burn down my ranch?"

"I'm not...I'm...I certainly didn't do this on purpose," she defended herself, lurching upright once again. "You startled me by sneaking up on me."

"You're saying this is my fault?"

Alexis couldn't make out his features very well, but there was no mistaking the anger in his voice and the furious thrust of his jaw. "I'm only saying I was startled,'' she shot back, beginning to grow angry herself. "I was trying to find my way to the house, and..."

"Carrying an open flame?"

"I don't have a flashlight. Making a torch was all I could think of to do after I knocked over that mailbox and ran into the wall."

"You knocked over the..." With a strangled sound, he stalked behind the car and stood staring down at the shattered pole and the mailbox that now pointed skyward. The other two men followed and the three of them stood shaking their heads and speaking in low tones.

After a moment, the first man stomped back to her. "Who are you? Do I have enemies somewhere that I don't know about and they sent you here to burn me out?"

"Oh, of course not," she said, her annoyance growing. "I don't know if you have any enemies or not. I don't even know who you are. I was looking for Mr. McTaggart. Mr. Jace McTaggart."

"Well, you found him," the man snapped. He clapped his hands onto his hips and thrust his jaw forward.

Alexis's heart plummeted to the scorched soles of her sneakers. She leaned forward and squinted at him, but she could barely see his face. What she saw didn't look very promising.

"You're...you're Mr. McTaggart, the head...the head of the Sleepy River school board?"

"Yes, heaven help us, I am."

"Oh." Of course, she thought. Why not an attempt

at arson to cap off this long, miserable day? Week? Month?

She didn't fold easily, though. Three hundred years of royal blood flowed in her veins. Her ancestors had once held out for three weeks against Napoleon's forces. Her grandfather had personally buried much of the royal treasury in a farmer's field rather than surrender it to the Nazis. She could handle this.

With the regal nod she'd copied from her grandmother, she held out her hand and said, "How do you do? I'm Alexis Chastain, the new schoolteacher."

Jace squinted through the darkness. "Alexis...?"

"Chastain," she supplied. "I'm here to teach at Sleepy River Community School."

He leaned forward and stared into her face, though he couldn't see much even with the help of the moonlight. "No. I don't know who you are, or what you're trying to pull, but the teacher we've hired is named Rachel Burrows and she's..."

"Not coming," the woman said firmly. "I'm here instead."

This was a nightmare, Jace assured himself firmly. The past few minutes when he'd awakened to the sound of a car stopping, followed by a muffled thump and splintering of wood, jumped into his clothes, and dashed outside to find a strange—emphasis on the word strange—woman holding a flaming torch were all part of the nightmare. He blinked, ran his hand over his face, and looked around. No. It all looked too real. Maybe he wasn't dreaming. Whatever was going on, he had to figure it out because this was his ranch. He was responsible for it and everyone on it. Jace took a deep breath. "What do you mean that you're here instead?"

"Rachel couldn't come, so I'm taking her place." She gave a firm little nod.

"No, no, no." He shook his head. "That's not how it works. See, how it works is that the school board interviews then hires a teacher who arrives when the contract says, and...what's the matter?"

The woman, the one with the fancy name of Alexis Chastain, was copying the way he shook his head as she said, "I told you, she can't come so I'm taking her place."

"That's impossible," Jace began with heat and not a little frustration. "You can't do that...."

"Boss," one of the other men broke in. "Does this have to be decided now? Can't we go into the house? It's near midnight and she looks about ready to drop."

Jace looked over at the brothers who'd worked for him since graduating from high school just over a year ago. He couldn't see much in the gloom, but he knew Rocky was the one who'd spoken. No doubt, Gil was nodding in agreement. He glanced back at the woman. He didn't think she looked ready to drop. Her hands were on her hips, her spine was straight as a railroad spike, and if she tipped forward, that outthrust chin of hers would spear him in the chest. As far as he could tell, she looked ready to argue.

"Okay," he said finally, giving her a wary look. "Gil, can you get this car out of here and park it up by the barn? Miss Chastain, give Gil your key and he'll take care of the car for you.''

He was glad to see that she obeyed without question, meekly handing over the car key to Gil, who quickly started the vehicle and pulled away. Jace winced at the sound of metal scraping against the wall, then against the broken mailbox post, but Gil gave an apologetic wave and disappeared up the long, graveled driveway.

"I'll put the hose away." Jace took the end of the garden hose from Rocky and began looping it as he did a rope. He didn't need to do this, but he always thought better if his hands were busy with something. What was he supposed to do with her? he thought furiously as he made loops in the plastic hose. Why hadn't that Rachel Burrows girl they'd hired shown up as she'd promised? She'd signed a contract. Didn't that mean anything? Blast it, he didn't want to deal with this. He hadn't even wanted to be head of the school board. He didn't have kids. He would probably never even have kids. Why should he need to do the job?

Because it was his turn. In a community as small as Sleepy River, everyone took a turn at some job. This year, Jace was head of the school board.

Disgruntled, he nodded toward the other man. "Rocky, you take her up to the house."

"I'll go get your bag for you, miss," Rocky said. "As soon as Gil parks your car for you."

"Oh, that's not necessary," she said, and Jace could hear determination in her voice. She turned and stumbled around until she located her purse on the ground. She hitched the strap over her shoulder as she said, "I can take care of everything myself. If you'll point me to the cottage I'm to occupy, I'll be fine."

Obviously, she thought that once she got inside the teacher's cottage, they couldn't dislodge her.

"It's not ready," Jace said.

"Not ready?" Now he heard a thread of panic in her voice. Hands thrust out, she turned from one to the other of them. "What do you mean?"

"You weren't...I mean, Miss Burrows wasn't expected until next week. No one's lived in the cottage for a couple of years. It needs to be cleaned. No, I've got a guest room. You'll stay there until we get this straightened out."

She opened her mouth as if to argue further, but then snapped it shut. Rocky could be a gentleman when he wanted to and he turned on the charm now as he said, "Don't you worry about a thing, miss. We'll get you settled in and things will look a lot better in the morning." Quickly, he took her arm and supported her as he guided her toward the ranch house. Jace could hear him talking quietly all the while, much as he did to a skittish filly.

Even as he wondered what in blazes he was going to do now, Jace finished winding up the hose and followed Rocky and Alexis to the house. Gil joined him as he reached the porch steps and the two of them walked inside together.

Jace nearly stumbled over his own size twelve feet at the sight that greeted him in the living room. Beside him, he heard Gil draw in his breath, and then choke out a cough.

Rocky was transfixed by the woman who stood, blinking in the glare of the overhead light Jace had flipped on when he'd run from the house. She didn't notice the men because she was busy inspecting the very masculine-looking living room.

A sideways glance at Gil told Jace that he, too, was thunderstruck. Jace wouldn't have been surprised to see the boys' eyes begin to slowly twirl cartoonlike in their heads. Their jaws had gone slack. Jace hoped they didn't start drooling.

He couldn't blame them, though, he thought as his own gaze was drawn back to her. She was a beauty all right, he admitted grudgingly.

Curly chestnut hair cascaded to a slim waist. Her face was fine-boned with almond-shaped green eyes and lips as luscious as a fresh peach. She wore sage green slacks and a matching cotton sweater that, even streaked with soot, made her look cool and unruffled.

A feeling he hoped was dread stirred within him. Great, he thought. Just great. It didn't matter what she called herself. He already knew her name. It was Trouble.

All this room needed was a chair made out of steer horns and cowhides, Alexis thought. The furnishings were dark, covered in scarred leather or faded Mexican serapes. There was a huge rag rug on the floor to lighten the somber mood of the room. For all its masculinity, the room felt invitingly comfortable. In fact, she wouldn't mind curling up on that old sofa right now and falling asleep—after crying her eyes out for half an hour.

A low noise that sounded like undisguised irritation broke off her interest in the living room. She turned to see all three men staring at her. To her surprise, she realized Gil and Rocky were twins. They appeared to be in their late teens or early twenties, with dark eyes and thick black hair that looked as if it needed attention from a barber who knew his way around a haystack. Both men were staring at her as if they were in a trance. She'd had that look turned on her before and she automatically began to stiffen her spine and give them a cool look, but then she realized that they only saw her as an attractive woman, not as a marriageable princess. Gratefully, she gave them a warm smile that seemed to buckle their knees.

"Gwarp," they said in unison and leaned on each other for strength.

Laughing softly, she looked at Jace McTaggart who was scowling ferociously. Her amusement died an instant death. This most definitely was not a man to be charmed. In fact, right now he looked mad enough to spit bullets.

Everything about him looked tough. He could fit right into an old western movie where it was often hard to tell heroes from villains.

This man could have played on either side of the law.

He was tall, at least six feet two, with broad shoulders that strained the seams of a white T-shirt, muscular arms and big hands that rested now at the waist of unbelted jeans that rode low on his hips.

His face would have invited comment anywhere.

His dark brown eyes were deep-set and searching, his nose was long and straight over a firm mouth. Even his hair, as dark and rich as mahogany, was straight, swept away from his broad forehead, and precisely cut. It was as if nature had put him together using a ruler and T-square, leaving off any softening effects. She felt a jolt of dismay, followed by a surge of warmth when his eyes lifted to meet hers.

"Miss Chastain," he began. "You don't belong here, but we'll discuss that in the morning. Right now Rocky is going to fetch your bag while Gil shows you to the guest room." He nodded toward the back of the house. "It's right through there and it has its own bathroom." He gave his two young employees a significant look. "As well as a lock on the door. Feel free to use it."

Alexis wanted to argue, to tell him she certainly belonged here, but she was too tired. "All right," she said with a meekness that surprised her.

"Rocky. Gil," Jace said. "Get moving."

The two men finally seemed to come out of their trances. With a blush, Rocky turned and plunged toward the front door, but was brought up short by the sight of a pile of rags beside it.

"Hey, Jace," he said, bending to pick it up. Alexis recognized it as the blanket she'd grabbed off the front porch. "What's this?"

Jace glanced at it. "That's what Miss Chastain grabbed to fight the fire she started."

She gave him a disgruntled look. She thought she'd done pretty well to find *something* to use.

Rocky held it up and she could see that it was an

old quilt, streaked now with dirt and mud, and with long scorch marks running its length. "But isn't this…?"

Jace's direct gaze swung back to Alexis. "The heirloom quilt my great-grandmother made out of her wedding dress," he said.

When she shut the guest room door behind her five minutes later, Alexis's face was still burning with embarrassment.

How could she possibly have known that quilt was an heirloom? And what on earth had it been doing lying on a chair on the front porch if it was so important? Her family certainly never left such things thrown around, she thought self-righteously. Not that it would be easy to do so with one of the fifteenth-century tapestries that filled her family home.

Still, Alexis felt terrible about the ruined quilt and she knew she'd need to make up for it somehow, along with any other fire damage she had caused.

This was not an auspicious beginning to her new job.

She was too tired to think about that right now. Reaching up, she rubbed her temples with her fingertips, then looked at the room which was hers for the night.

Like the rest of the house, it was decidedly masculine. The bed had an old-fashioned iron bed frame and a high mattress covered with a black-and-blue plaid bedspread. A fifties-style lamp with a tiered shade in Chinese red stood on a rickety table that had been painted a cheerful yellow. A faded rag rug much like the one in the living room covered an oval section of floor beside the bed.

The riotous color scheme didn't matter to her. Cleanliness was the most important thing and this room definitely looked clean. Stark, she thought with a grim smile as she set her suitcase on the bed and flipped it open, but certainly clean.

Delighted with the luxury of a private bathroom, Alexis quickly prepared for bed, then climbed gratefully between the covers. Even as she drifted off to sleep, she pictured Jace McTaggart's face as he'd told her she didn't belong in Sleepy River.

Tomorrow she would prove him wrong, she thought as she drifted into exhausted sleep. She appeared to be on some kind of quest to prove a number of people wrong. She might as well add him to the list.

Alexis thought of his snapping dark eyes, firm jaw, and emphatic statement that she didn't belong. In fact, she would put him at the top of the list.

Chapter Two

Pounding on the bedroom door and a loud male voice announcing, "Breakfast in ten minutes," had Alexis springing upright as if the palace guards had shot off a cannon over her head.

Hand clutched to her throat, she looked around wildly for Esther before she realized that her lady-in-waiting wasn't there and she wasn't in her own apartments in the palace.

It was several more seconds before her mind cleared enough to tell her that she was in Sleepy River, Arizona, where she had run for a temporary refuge from family tensions and responsibilities.

Exhaling a relieved sigh, she looked around and was pleased to see that the room didn't seem quite as dauntingly colorful as it had the night before. In fact, the furnishings held a somewhat eclectic charm. The cheerful August sun streaming in the east-facing windows helped a great deal, sending a warm glow across the foot of the bed, the wooden floor and the cozy rug.

Alexis yawned, stretched and stared at her bedside clock. Even though she'd barely had six hours of sleep, she felt refreshed. More than that, she felt eager. She would begin preparing for her new job today—as soon as she had convinced her reluctant host/school board chairman that her presence there was no mistake.

She slipped out of bed and walked over to the window. Blinking in the bright morning sunlight, she gazed out at the view, and was pleasantly surprised to see an open pasture dotted with cattle in the distance. Towering pine, aspen and spruce trees covered the upslope of the nearest mountain and a fruit orchard grew nearby.

It was a lovely, pastoral scene marred only by the faint, lingering stench of burned grass from last night's fire.

Wincing at the memory of her clumsiness, Alexis pulled away from the window and wondered how she was going to make up for that fiasco. Half-smiling, she remembered what her mother used to say, "Sometimes, all one can do is hold the head high and keep going, saying nothing."

Somehow, Alexis didn't think that Jace followed that philosophy.

What had he said? Ten minutes? Alexis glanced at the clock again. And she'd already wasted three. She scurried out of bed, grabbed some clothes from her suitcase and dashed for the bathroom.

* * *

Jace looked dubiously around the breakfast table. Rocky and Gil had arrived earlier than usual. Since Jace was the best cook of the three of them, he cooked breakfast while Gil and Rocky did some outside chores, then came in, unshaven, grizzled and already dusty, to eat eggs, toast and bacon and slurp coffee while they discussed the day's work.

This morning, though, they hadn't been able to make it outside for any chores because they'd been busy fighting over use of the bathroom. Jace had heard the unaccustomed weekday sounds of a couple of buzzing electric razors. He was then treated to the sight of his two hired men arriving in the kitchen with slicked-down hair, clean shirts, jeans and boots, wearing enough aftershave and cologne to knock over a nine-hundred-pound steer.

"You two boys going somewhere?" he'd asked, staring first at one, then the other of them.

"Nah," they'd answered in harmony, then shuffled their feet and sat down. In unison, they turned to stare, unblinking, at the new schoolteacher's bedroom door. They reminded him of a couple of coyotes waiting outside a prairie dog's den for the tasty morsel to appear.

When her bedroom door did open and she emerged, Alexis jumped back immediately, alarmed by the rush of two large male bodies in her direction. The cowboys bowed before her and she threw Jace an alarmed look over their bobbing heads. He fought a grin, pleased to see that for all her boldness, these two hired hands could perturb her.

"Morning, Miss Chastain," Gil said, grinning like a fool as he rose from his sweeping bow.

"Did you sleep well, miss?" Rocky asked, elbowing his brother aside.

Gil placed his booted foot in front of Rocky's, reached out with his own elbow, and gave his brother a poke in the ribs that had Rocky's eyes bugging from their sockets as he made a strangled sound.

"F...fine," she stammered, looking at Jace's two crazed cowboys and then at him as if trying to figure out which way to run.

"Boys," he said mildly, strolling across the kitchen to take charge. "Quit crowding the lady. Let her sit down and have some breakfast." He looked at her and nodded toward the table.

She gave him a wobbly smile that had him focusing on her. Last night, he had been too caught up in his surprise and annoyance to notice much beyond her knockout looks and her insistence that she had come to stay.

Now, he saw that she had courage, as well, because these two idiot cowboys hadn't sent her shrieking back to her room. She also had compassion because she was still smiling at Gil and Rocky. Jace felt his interest in her growing and he didn't like that at all. He frowned at the boys so furiously, they leaped to do his bidding.

"Oh, oh yeah, sure Jace." They both stood back, still grinning, as she skirted cautiously around them. As she reached to pull out a chair, the boys seemed to recall their manners and, as one, vaulted to do it for her. She saw them coming and managed to dart aside just in time to avoid being flattened in the rush. As it was, they tripped over each other, hissed a few expletives into each other's ears, and had a minor skirmish, but they eventually dragged the chair out. They gazed at Alexis like a couple of puppies waiting for a treat. Jace decided it was time he took matters in hand.

"You two sit down," he ordered them. "You're scaring the hel…heck out of her," he growled. For a moment, he considered telling one of them to pour her some coffee, but realized that putting anything hot into their hands at this moment was just asking for trouble.

He poured some for himself, and when he held up the pot inquiringly, she nodded and gave him a nervous smile as she seated herself.

There was a moment of awkward hesitation before Gil and Rocky realized they were supposed to be passing food and hurriedly grabbed for platters of toast and eggs which they shoved at Alexis. Bewildered, she reached jerkily for them before the contents sailed down her shirtfront.

Jace sighed. It was a good thing she would be leaving today or they would never get any more work done. He might be hoping for something that wasn't going to happen, though. The real teacher they'd hired, Rachel Burrows, was only slightly less attractive than this woman.

Still, he'd better send her on her way directly after breakfast because Gil and Rocky had some branding to do and the way things were going, they'd be decorating each other's rumps with the Running M brand.

He sipped his coffee as his gaze drifted over the bright red-brown fall of her hair. It cascaded down her back and contrasted with the pale gold camp shirt she wore with a pair of faded jeans. The combination of colors made him think of fall leaves, but her green eyes looked like spring.

When he realized what direction his thoughts were taking, Jace choked on a sip of coffee and coughed several times. Alexis gave him a concerned look, but neither Gil nor Rocky spared him a glance. They were so enthralled with her that he could have dropped dead on the tabletop and they would have done no more than reach across his cold, stiff body to get the butter for her. Obviously, it was time he got this situation under control.

"Miss Chastain, we appreciate you stopping by," he began lamely. "But there's been a mistake. You're not the one we hired for the teaching position, so we'll just wait until Miss Burrows comes, and..."

"But she's not coming," Alexis interrupted, blinking those big green eyes at him.

Gil and Rocky turned and stared at him as if he'd suddenly begun singing soprano. He ignored them.

"Not coming?"

"That's what I was trying to tell you last night. You see, Rachel and I are old friends, college roommates, in fact. On her way here, she came to visit me at the pal...place...at my place, and said she had this job, but was going to have to call and resign from her contract, so I came instead."

Jace stared at her for a long moment, trying and failing to take this in. He leaned forward on one elbow and stared at her. In a dead-level voice he said, "She signed a contract. When a person signs a contract, they're supposed to fulfill it, at least that's the way the rest of the world does it."

"Uh, yes." A nervous smile fluttered across those full lips. "And she feels really terrible about not being able to fulfill it, but something...came up. Something very important, and she can't come. I have a letter from her, though," Alexis added eagerly. "We thought it would get here faster if I brought it rather than depending on the postal system. I'll go get it."

She scooted back in preparation for a dash to her room. As soon as she moved, Gil and Rocky were on their feet to assist her. Another scuffle ensued while they fought over her chair. The tenuous hold Jace had on his temper snapped like a stretched elastic band.

"Will you two please eat your breakfast and get out of here?" Jace roared. "You're so jumpy you'd make a snail nervous." They gaped at him and bounced back into their chairs. "Miss Chastain, why don't you just tell me why she didn't come, what came up that was so important?"

Alexis met his gaze, which was beginning to look mighty scary. This was what she'd been afraid of. Oh, he looked big and intimidating and very, very businesslike this morning. It didn't help that he also looked virile and manly, and slightly disreputable with a day's growth of beard shadowing his jaw.

It would have been so much easier if Rachel had handled this in a professional manner, calling and talking to Jace in person, but she'd been afraid of a lawsuit, of being talked into coming here when her heart had been somewhere else, that she'd ducked her responsibility. So Alexis was covering for her. It wasn't the first time she'd done it. Covering up for people was an old habit of hers because she hated to see her loved ones hurt. Besides, Rachel was a rare commodity, a true friend who'd never spilled anything about Alexis or her family to a tabloid.

She drew in a deep breath and looked at the hard, curious face of the man sitting across the breakfast table from her. She had to tell him the truth about Rachel.

She glanced around the kitchen, at Gil and Rocky, and then back at him. Nope. No way out of it. Finally, she picked up her cup and mumbled something into it.

"What? She *what* someone?"

Alexis took a sip of coffee, cleared her throat, then beamed a high-voltage smile at him. "She met someone."

"Someone? You mean a man?"

"Oh, not just any man. Her soul mate."

"Soul mate." The two words dropped into the atmosphere like stones thumping into mud.

"At least that's what she said. It was love at first sight. She couldn't leave him." Boy, oh boy did that sound lame, and unprofessional, and well, a little stupid. Alexis sighed. "It's not as bad as it sounds...."

"She's not here to fulfill her teaching contract because she met her soul mate and she can't leave his side. Does that about cover it?" he asked testily.

Alexis attempted a smile. "Well, it sounded a little more romantic when she said it."

He glowered at her.

She started to her feet once again. "I'll go get the letter and you can read…"

"Sit down," he growled.

She plopped back into her chair.

Gil—at least she was pretty sure it was Gil— dragged his gaze away from her face long enough to ask, "What difference does it make, Jace, as long as we have a qualified teacher to teach the kids?"

"Yeah," Rocky agreed. "Miss Chastain here is obviously well-qualified."

Jace raised a brow at him. Rocky's eyes were glued on a part of her anatomy that had nothing whatsoever to do with her teaching ability. Blushing, Alexis crossed her arms over her chest.

Leaning forward, Jace said, "Why don't you two go out and get to work? I need to talk to her alone."

Alexis saw the twins look at their boss as if he'd suggested they hop in the truck and run over their favorite pet. Jace jerked his head toward the barn.

Grumbling, his two men cleared their places, took their dishes to the sink, and then trooped out glumly, but over his shoulder, Gil said, "Just don't do anything stupid."

When they were gone, Jace said, "What I don't like here is the unprofessional way this has been handled, and the fact that I feel that I, and the other members of the school board, are being manipulated."

"Um yes, I understand that." What could she say? That she had jumped at the chance offered by her old roommate because she wanted to get away from home? No, that would really make her sound desperate. And she certainly couldn't tell him that "home" was a two-hundred room palace situated in one of the most beautiful valleys in Europe.

"Well, then you understand that you have to leave?"

She blinked at him. "No, I mean I understand how you might feel manipulated." Quickly, she leaned forward and placed her hands on the tabletop, palms up in a pleading gesture. "I truly am a qualified teacher. I'm certified by the state of Arizona, I've done my student teaching. I can do this job."

He lifted a thick, dark eyebrow at her as he shook his head. "No, this won't work."

"School starts in less than two weeks," she said desperately. "Where are you going to find someone else at the last minute? I'm here. I'm available. I want to do the job. Please let me stay."

She had made her plea too heartfelt. Now he was staring at her with open curiosity. "Why do you want it so badly?"

She paused as her mind scrambled for an answer. Anxious perspiration popped out on her top lip. "Why?" she stalled, giving him her most guileless look.

He crossed his arms on the tabletop and stared at her. "That's right. Why? If you're so qualified, why do you want to work here? And on a job that will only last one semester?"

Because things will have cooled down at home in four months. Her father would have a new project going and would have the let's-marry-off-Alexis light out of his eyes. And because Alexis would be at least partly over her anger and disappointment with her father. While Prince Michael had been wrangling with his national council, revising the constitution of Inbourg, she had stayed quietly at home as he had requested, supporting him, helping run the household and taking care of her nephew Jean Louis while Anya and Deirdre had been Prince Michael's ambassadors to the country and to the world.

She didn't do any of the things she had planned like living on her own and working on her master's degree in education so she could help bring the schools of Inbourg up to a higher standard. As soon as the constitution was rewritten and approved, her father had turned his attention to her and begun making sweeping statements about it being time for her to marry. She was the steady, sensible one who wouldn't make a foolish marriage as Anya had done with her race car driver, nor would she be a flirt like Deirdre. She knew her father loved her, but she also knew he didn't see her as the professional she wanted to be.

"Did you forget the question?" Jace asked, bringing her attention back to him.

"While it's true that Rachel and I have gone about this job switch in a somewhat…" She flashed him a glance. "…unconventional way, you have nothing to worry about."

Jace raised an eyebrow at her again. He was really very good at that, she thought nervously. He could exhibit rank skepticism with the twitch of a few muscles.

"Unconventional?" he asked.

Realizing she wasn't getting anywhere with this tactic, Alexis said, "I want to work here because I need the experience," she said honestly. "It's a job I'm qualified for." She stood. "I'll get Rachel's letter and my references as well as a copy of my state certification. You can judge for yourself."

She sped to her room, grabbed her papers and was back in a flash. Somewhat breathlessly, she handed them to him and while he read them, she hung over his shoulder anxiously. "Rachel's letter explains everything. She says how sorry she is, and that she knows me and my qualifications, and..."

"I can read it for myself," Jace grumbled, giving her a steady look that had her backing off.

Chastened, she sat down and ate a few more bites of her breakfast and had a couple of sips of coffee. For the first time since the meal began, she paid real attention to the food. The bacon was perfectly cooked and, before they'd grown cold on her plate, the scrambled eggs had been moist and fluffy. Had Jace prepared this meal?

She glanced up to see the way he was examining Rachel's letter of resignation. His angular face was lined in a mighty frown. In the long, third floor gallery of her family's palace there was a painting of an ancestor who'd been rumored to put to death those who disappointed him. Right now, Jace's face looked a great deal like that painting.

He put down the letter and picked up the folder

with Alexis's certificate and letters of reference. She bounced up and hurried around the table to hover at his shoulder once again.

In a hearty voice, she said, "See? I'm fully qualified." She pointed to the date on her certificate. "For at least the next seven years."

Jace answered with a grunting sound and picked up one of the letters.

"And see?" She crowded him as she pressed forward over his shoulder. "This says that I have specialized training in diagnosing and solving reading difficulties."

He gave her another one of those "back-off" looks and asked, "Do you have any training in washing dishes?"

Alexis stared blankly into his deep brown eyes for a few seconds, then looked at the dirty plates and cups on the table. She straightened immediately. "Oh, of course. Um, you'd like to read these things without me chattering away at you, wouldn't you?"

"Yes." He stood and gathered them up. "And I need to talk to the other members of the school board."

Hope flooded her face and joy sparkled in her eyes. "You mean there's a chance you'll change your mind and let me stay?"

"I mean I'll talk to the other members of the school board."

She would have to be satisfied with that, so she swallowed the little lump of disappointment and gave him a bright smile as she held up her hands, palms outward, "Fine. Fine. Go right ahead."

"I intend to." He turned away. "I'll be in my office."

Before he left the kitchen, Alexis took a quick look around. "Um, where's the dishwasher?"

For the first time, she saw a hint of amusement in his face. His craggy features rearranged themselves into what must pass for a smile. Taking a step back to her, he reached out and lifted her hand by the wrist. He held it in front of her face and said, "You're looking at it, kid."

She started at the hard warmth of his touch and her gaze flew to meet his. Wide-eyed, she stared at him. Why had he done that?

The flash of humor she'd seen vanished. Jace looked into her eyes as if he was asking himself the same question. Hastily, he dropped her hand and turned to stride from the kitchen. "I have to make some phone calls."

When he was gone, Alexis stared blindly around the room, then moved to clear the table. Why had he touched her? She found it vaguely disturbing. It made her think of him as someone other than a boss, someone she had to convince to let her stay. His touch made her think of him as a man.

Silly, she thought. She was overreacting, that was all. Just fearful that he wouldn't let her stay. Pushing her disturbing thoughts away, she began clearing the table.

"Jace, I think you're overreacting," Martha Singleton told him in a flat tone.

"You do?" Jace sat with his elbows propped on

the desk as he talked to the woman who was the regular teacher of Sleepy River Community School—on the years she wasn't having a baby.

"Yes. First of all, where are we going to find someone at this late date? If the one we hired didn't show up and another, qualified teacher did, I don't see that we have anything to worry about. Check her references. If they're okay, she's okay. Believe me when I say qualified teachers willing to teach in a one-room schoolhouse in the mountains for the amount of money we can pay aren't exactly thick on the ground."

Jace scratched his chin. "I guess you're right," he said in a reluctant drawl. He paused and he could feel Martha waiting for him to go on. In the background, he could hear her three-week-old son fussing, wanting his mother's attention.

"So, what is the problem, then?" she asked.

Jace knew she was too polite to say so, but he was wasting her time. "No problem," he said, with more decisiveness than he felt. "I'll check her references. Sounds like you need to get back to that baby of yours."

"Demanding little stinker," she said fondly. "Tell you what, if her references check out okay, but you're still worried, I can go watch her teach. If she's totally incompetent, we don't have to keep her."

It was a slim thread, but Jace grasped it gratefully. "Sure, Martha. That sounds good. We don't want a teacher who's incompetent."

Only he had a feeling Alexis wasn't incompetent.

Jace hung up the phone and gloomily stared out the window in the direction of the schoolhouse.

In spite of her tendency to run into walls, back into mailbox posts and set fires, there was something about her that seemed capable of handling anything, even the challenges of their local school.

Admit it, sucker, he thought. It wasn't her capabilities that worried him. It was her presence, the way she had looked at him a little while ago as if she'd never seen anything like him. No doubt, she hadn't. To him, she appeared to be accustomed to much more sophisticated surroundings than Sleepy River, Arizona.

She disturbed him, had done so since the moment he'd looked into those eyes of hers. Touching her hand had rocked him back on his heels.

He was reluctant to have her around, but as Martha had said, where were they going to find someone else at this late date? Grumbling, he reached for the phone to contact her references.

Why did it have to be Alexis Chastain, though?

Chapter Three

"**O**kay, the job's yours," Jace said abruptly half an hour later.

Alexis started and turned from the sink where she'd been rinsing the dishcloth after wiping down the counter for the sixth time. She'd had to fight the temptation to listen at the door of his office. In fact, she'd begun tiptoeing in that direction, but a squeaking floorboard in the dining room had announced itself loudly and sent her scurrying back to the kitchen.

Resigned to wait, she had instead done the washing up, wiped the table and the counter and swept the floor. Her sisters, and most of the people employed at the palace, would have howled with laughter at the sight. Bevins, the palace manager, who'd been an English butler in another life, would have been appalled. Esther, her lady-in-waiting, would have called for smelling salts.

"I do?" she asked with a delighted grin.

"Looks like it," he responded with a shrug.

"Thank you. That's wonderful. I'm so glad." Alexis stepped forward excitedly and reached out to shake his hand. She'd forgotten to put down the dish-cloth, though, so he got a fistful of wet rag. He grimaced and her face flushed scarlet.

"Oh! I'm sorry," she cried, turning away to throw it into the sink. They both wiped damp hands on their jeans while she gave him an apologetic look.

"As I was saying," Jace nodded toward the papers he'd laid on the edge of the table. "Your references checked out, though a couple of them seemed to think it was pretty funny to hear you wanted a job here."

Nervousness fluttered in her stomach. Alexis folded her hands and gave him a cautious look. "They did?"

"Especially one of your professors who said he thought you were in Europe." He gave her a sharply inquisitive look as he raised a dark brow. Again he reminded her of that painting in the palace's long gallery. It took her a second, but she finally recalled that ancestor's name. Hedrick. They'd called him Hedrick the Henchman.

Her gaze skittered away from Jace's. If she remembered correctly, Hedrick had been fond of the technology of the time, most significantly, anything to do with the latest thing in torture devices.

"Were you?"

She blinked at him. "Was I what?"

"In Europe."

"Oh, that. Yes. Yes, I was. Family business."

He gave her another measured look. "Exactly what kind of business is your family in?"

Alexis's smile froze. Her mind scrambled over scenes of the past months; her father working with the national council late into the night, her sisters making endless rounds of social gatherings to convince the people of their tiny country that the changes Prince Michael wanted would be the best for everyone. Alexis, herself, shunning the spotlight and staying behind to watch out for young Jean Louis, her nephew, eventual heir to the throne, and an unrepentant con artist and charmer who was able to convince everyone in the palace from his nanny to the guards at the front gates that it was perfectly acceptable behavior for a six-year-old to attempt to hang by his shoe tips from an upstairs window so he could "see everything upside down."

"Alexis?" Jace prompted.

She glanced up. "Public relations..." she blurted. "...and government work. I chose to take a leave from the family business and pursue my real interest, which is teaching." Inwardly, she winced at the half truth. Her "leave" had actually been a bit less forthright than that since she had told her father she was going to a spa in Arizona for an extended stay.

Prince Michael, who considered his daughters' purpose in life to be purely decorative, anyway, hadn't objected to her visit since he assumed she was planning to make herself even more alluring in order to appeal to one of the young men he would soon begin parading before her. The thought of that old-fashioned idea made her fume. She wouldn't think about that right now, though.

Jace opened his mouth to say something, but she barreled ahead. "Now that you've decided I can stay, why don't you show me to the school, so I can get started? There's a great deal to be done before the first day."

She held her breath, thinking he was going to question her further, but after a long moment in which he seemed to be trying to see right inside her head, he nodded slowly and said, "All right. You can drive your car over there and park it by the teacherage."

Relieved, she nodded and broke into a wide smile that made her face glow. "Teacherage," she breathed in delight. "That sounds so…"

"Old-fashioned," he supplied with a lift of his brow. "Out-of-date?"

"Respectable," she answered and saw surprise flicker in his eyes. "Remember that in the days of the Old West, the local teacher was the one people came to for information or to have disputes settled."

This time his eyes narrowed and he gave her another long look. She wished he wouldn't do that. It was unnerving. A lifetime of adeptness at hiding her thoughts seemed to do no good around him.

"You don't think you're in the Old West, do you?"

"No, of course not." Alexis clasped her hands at her waist. She didn't know how she could explain what she meant. If she told him how delighted she was to have the job, to be living in this remote corner of Arizona away from prying eyes and from her well-meaning but meddling family, he might become suspicious of her and her abilities.

Evasively, she cleared her throat. "Well, never mind that." She turned away from his too-penetrating gaze and said, "Let me get my things and I'll be right with you." She dashed to her room where she grabbed her things, made sure the place was neat, and then met Jace outside.

One of the twins had brought her car around front and she was dismayed to see the dent she'd put in the back fender. At least only a few people knew about it, she thought, with the instinctive reaction of someone whose family had long been stalked by the paparazzi. In Inbourg, the accident would have been front page news in their tiny weekly newspaper. In Sleepy River, it hardly mattered. She knew Rachel would trust her to have the damage repaired.

Jace drove by in a dark blue pickup truck and called out, "Follow me," as he passed.

She doubted that he would be willing to wait long, so Alexis tumbled into her car and followed, wincing at the sight of the burned area of grass. She sincerely hoped it would grow back quickly and the near-disaster would be forgotten. Of course, there was still the matter of what to do about the heirloom quilt she'd ruined, but she decided to worry about that another time. She was determined to handle her problems like one of those American television martial arts experts handled the bad guys—one at a time.

Halfway down the lane leading to the highway, Jace turned off on a road she hadn't noticed the night before. Through towering trees that almost scraped the sides of the car, they emerged into an open field that held a small white schoolhouse, an even smaller cottage and a baseball diamond.

Alexis's happy gaze swept the area, then lighted dubiously on the ball field. She hoped no one expected her to coach baseball. She knew very little about it. Tennis, now, that was something she could coach, but she didn't think she'd be called on to do so.

Her eyes were drawn back to the school and teacherage, pleased that everything looked to be in good repair. She stopped the car and bounced out, then up the ramp that led to the front door of the school.

Jace had stepped from his truck and was following her actions with puzzlement. "Don't you want to see where you're going to live?"

"Later," she said, waving her hand airily. She tried the knob and found that it was locked. "Do you have the key?"

"I'm the school board president," he grumbled, following her. "Of course, I've got the key."

He sounded so grumpy, Alexis had to resist the urge to laugh. Instead, she stood back and let him open the door and push it open for her. When Jace stood back, she stepped inside and took an excited scan of the place.

"Oh, this is much more modern than I'd expected," she said, seeing the teacher's desk in the corner, a double row of students' desks, supply cabinets and a line of computers along one wall.

"What did you expect?" Jace asked. "Teacher's desk on a raised platform? A wood-burning stove in the corner?'' He chuckled. "A two-holer outhouse instead of a rest room?''

A blush washed over her cheeks as she glanced at him. He was teasing her. And that sound he'd made. Could that have been a laugh? She gave him a smile and he seemed to recall who she was—the woman who'd set fire to his grass. He scowled.

"I'm only surprised that there's such modern equipment up here in the mountains.'' She indicated the row of computers. "This will make my job much easier.''

Jace gave her an interested look. "You know quite a bit about using these things, hmm?''

She stepped forward to open a cabinet and was pleased to see it was stacked neatly full of reams of paper and boxes of pencils. Absently, she answered him. "Yes. I've taken classes and I helped Bevins work up spreadsheets to keep track of expenses and make an inventory of the wine cellar.'' She glanced around at the bookcases full of textbooks and the open shelves of art supplies. She was becoming more and more excited about her first school. This was going to be wonderful. She could arrange her curriculum to take advantage of the students' real interests.

"Wine cellar?'' Jace asked in a level tone.

Alexis blinked. "What?'' The scowl on Jace's face had deepened.

"You said you helped Bevins inventory the wine cellar.''

"Oh, I did?'' Her hand fluttered up to fiddle with the collar of her shirt. Darn, why hadn't she been paying attention to what was coming out of her mouth?

"You did," he assured her. "Who's Bevins?"

She put her hands behind her back and rocked onto her toes nonchalantly as she avoided his gaze. "Oh, he's a man who's in charge of a very large wine cellar. Did you go to school here?" she asked brightly.

He frowned at her abrupt evasiveness and she sighed inwardly. He was becoming suspicious of her and there didn't seem to be anything she could do about it. Subtlety had never been her strongest trait, which was another reason she'd been kept out of the glare of publicity. Any nosy reporter asking her a question was likely to receive a rude response.

"Yes, I did, but eventually the school closed and we were bussed into Morenci. It was a long trip for all of us kids, and hard because we had chores. My dad wasn't one to let me off just because..."

Interested, Alexis stared into his dark eyes, seeing something flash in their brown depths. Was it regret? And was the regret because of those long bus trips of his childhood, followed by chores, or because he'd almost said something personal?

"Just because of what?" she prompted.

His frown deepened. "Never mind. It doesn't concern you."

Stung, she straightened. Obviously, subtlety wasn't his strong point, either.

Gifting him with the down-the-nose look that all good teachers develop early, she said, "Why don't you show me the house now? I might as well get settled in so I can start work."

Jace nodded and for an instant, she thought he looked relieved that she wasn't going to ask him any more questions. It annoyed her that he was so willing to ask them, but was unwilling to answer them.

However, given her own secrets, she couldn't complain. Besides, theirs was a working relationship, after all, not a friendly one. No matter how much he intrigued her, she needed to remember that.

She took her suitcase, which he easily lifted from her hand and carried up the steps to the tiny porch. A sturdy old Adirondack chair sat there, and she envisioned herself on fine fall evenings, sitting in it quietly enjoying the peace.

Jace unlocked the door and pushed it open, then handed her the key before stepping back to let her walk inside first. He seemed to realize immediately that it was a mistake because he cleared his throat and said, "Some of the mothers of the students intended to come clean the place before you—I mean—the other teacher arrived, but you came early."

"It's all right," she said quickly, glancing around. "I can do it." The living room contained a sagging leather-covered couch that looked perfect for afternoon naps, a couple of mismatched chairs, tables and lamps. It was as if everyone in the neighborhood had brought something in for the teacherage, but hadn't planned things out beforehand. She liked that.

Smiling, she walked through to the kitchen which besides the appliances, held a small table with two chairs. The bathroom was strictly utilitarian and the bedroom held only a bed and dresser. The mattress looked as though it had cornered the market on lumps, but she thought she could survive it for a few months.

When she didn't say anything, Jace seemed to feel the need to fill up the silence.

"No one's lived here in years," he said, walking around the living room, putting up the shades and opening the windows. "The regular teacher, Martha Singleton is married to a local rancher and has her own home." He looked around the room with dismay. Dust lay thick on every surface. "Not exactly a palace, is it?" he asked ruefully.

"No," Alexis answered firmly, thinking of the perfection Bevins maintained, the battles over repair budgets for the four-hundred-year-old structure that was her family home, the vast numbers of people who came and went at all hours of the day and night. "It certainly isn't."

He seemed to misunderstand the emphasis she'd put on the words. "It's the only place available," he told her with a hint of defensiveness. "I'm the closest neighbor to the school, but you can't live at my house. Rocky and Gil would never get a lick of work done. As it is, it'll probably take them a week to recover from breakfast this morning."

Insulted, she stared at him. "I was hardly trying to entice them, you know."

"You don't have to try," he said, throwing out a hand in a tight little gesture of frustration. "Having you around, having any woman around, throws everything off, and…" He broke off and ran a hand through his hair. "Oh, for crying…" He took a breath and lumbered on while she stared at him, open-mouthed. "If you're going to take the job, you have to stay here, at least until other arrangements can be made, though what those would be, I don't know."

She was beginning to get angry with him. "I never said this accommodation wasn't suitable. This is fine. Perfectly fine." For emphasis, she stomped across the room and flopped down on the sofa. A cloud of dust rose into the air, sending her into a coughing fit. Sneezing, she staggered to her feet, rubbing her itchy nose, and wiping her eyes. "It...ahchoo! Only needs a...a...ahchoo, a little cleaning." Attempting to regain her dignity, she swiped tears from her eyes and wheezed, "I don't need your help, but I'd like to...to...whoo...ahchoo, know one thing." That sneeze doubled her over, but she straightened and glared at him.

"What's that?" he asked warily, standing back from the line of fire she was maintaining with her sneezes.

"You have no children in the school, you don't seem to want anything to do with it. Why are you the president of the school board?"

"Because it's a small community and we have to take turns at the jobs. Last year, I had to be the one to deal with the county regarding our water pumping station. This year, that's Dave Kramer's job, and I'm school board president."

"Well, I certainly don't want to make your unwanted job harder, so I'll call on you as little as possible," she said primly. "Now that you've shown me inside, and given me the keys, I can take care of myself."

He raised an eyebrow at her as if to say, "That'll be the day." Instead, he answered, "All right, then. I'll go and let you get to work. The cupboards are stocked with dishes, pots and utensils, but you'll have to go into town to get food. I can send Gil or Rocky if you don't want..."

"I'll take care of it, thank you," she responded, lifting her chin. "I need to buy cleaning products, anyway."

Jace strode toward the door, then paused as if he was going to say something else, but then thought better of it. "Goodbye, then," he rapped out, and left, rattling the door in its frame and clumping across the porch.

Fool, he called himself once he was outside. Why had he made the idea of having her staying in his house sound like it would be a visit from Typhoid Mary? The truth was, that what with knocking down mailbox posts and setting fires, she'd livened the place up. He'd never seen his two hired hands so spiffed up for breakfast. It had made a nice change.

Jace headed for his truck, grabbed a pair of pliers and a wrench, and then made a U-turn and strode around to the back of the cottage to turn on her water and electricity, and make sure there was plenty of propane in the tank that supplied gas to her water heater and kitchen range.

As he wrenched the water valve open, he acknowledged that he'd snapped at her for the very same reason he'd tried to get rid of her earlier, because she unnerved him.

Well, he didn't have to see much of her, he assured

himself grimly. He would stay away from her, send one of his love-struck cowboys over to check on her. He was too damned busy, anyway, to spend time checking on the new schoolmarm, to trot over whenever she needed a nail hammered or a door unstuck. He had a ranch to run, for pity's sake, plenty to think about and do.

There was no way he was going to lope through the woods like a faithful puppy whenever she needed something. He would finish this little job, and then be gone. One of the other board members, Stella Kramer, for instance, could handle things from here on out. After all, she had three kids in the school, so she had a reason to keep the teacher happy.

His job finished, his mind made up, Jace picked up his tools and started for his truck. His decision to stay away from Alexis lasted all of five seconds and ended at the precise moment he heard her scream.

Chapter Four

"**W**hat's the matter?"

Alexis could hear Jace shouting to her as she sprinted out of the kitchen and into the living room. Panicked, she made a flying leap toward him. He caught her around the waist, then twirled her behind him as he searched the room for the threat.

"What is it, Alexis?" he asked, his gaze scanning the dusty room with its mismatched furniture.

"It's...it's in the kitchen. Something...a whole bunch of somethings...in the cupboard." Her breath came in quick, sharp struggles for air. Somehow her hands had fisted into the front of his shirt and she was holding on for all she was worth. A part of her mind told her she ought to let go, but she couldn't just yet.

"I'll take a look." Jace started forward, then seemed to realize they were attached at the chest. His dark eyes curious, he glanced down at her white-knuckled hands clenching his shirtfront. In a mild voice, he said, "Uh, Alexis, you're either going to have to let go or you're going to have to come back in there with me."

She stared into his face for a second. "What? Oh! Oh, no, I don't want to do…" Heat flooded her face as she finally managed to uncurl her fingers from the fabric of his shirt and step back. "Sorry." She cleared her throat. "I didn't realize I was… Sorry."

His eyes were serious, but she saw amusement kindling there. No doubt he now thought she was a nitwit as well as a firebug. She cleared her throat. "I'd appreciate it if you'd take a look." She couldn't quite meet his eyes so she stared at his mouth which seemed to be twitching in amusement. "I assure you that if it was some ordinary family of creatures I could deal with it, but obviously these are a rare sort of…of Arizona mountain varmint that…that requires your expertise."

His slight smile bloomed into a full grin. "Oh, really? Well, I'll go take a look and see if I can get rid of this bunch of varmints on my own, or if I'll need to call in all the neighbors and the Arizona National Guard."

She lifted her chin. "Thank you."

With a shake of his head, he started toward the kitchen.

"Jace," she quavered, stopping him.

"What?"

Alexis gulped, her eyes wide. "Be careful. Whatever those things are, they might be rabid. They *looked* rabid." She lifted her hands and formed them into claws. "Big yellow eyes. Even bigger yellow teeth."

The corner of his mouth crooked as if he was trying not to laugh, but he gave a single nod.

Cautiously, Alexis trailed along in his wake even as she berated herself for her ridiculous display of panic. She'd been surprised, that's all. And she really didn't deal well with little scurrying creatures who squawked and screeched when *they* were surprised. She lingered near the door.

In the kitchen, Jace stopped and cocked an eyebrow at her. "Which cupboard?"

"The one on the right-hand side of the sink, next to the window. Be careful," she warned again as he reached for the scarred old wooden door.

He cracked the door open and peeked inside. More scurrying followed and he quickly shut the cupboard, holding it firmly closed. "You're right," he said solemnly. "These are wild, dangerous mountain creatures. Living in these mountains has caused them to morph into vicious, feral beings the likes of which modern science has never seen."

Eyes wide, Alexis gulped. "Really? What...what are they?"

He dropped the solemn look and rolled his eyes. "Ordinary tree squirrels," he said. "Step back." When she did so, he stretched over to open the back door, then threw the cupboard door wide and banged the underside of the cabinet with his massive fist.

Three squirrels erupted from inside, chattering and screeching. They whirled through the kitchen, across the top of the counter and over the stove, fluffy tails flying, then made for the door. They disappeared outside and up the nearest pine tree where they sat, rudely scolding the humans who had dared to evict them.

Alexis rushed across the kitchen and closed the door firmly, then looked back at Jace who was examining the cabinet. Daylight shone through the back. "They chewed a hole through the outside of the house," he said. "Then set up housekeeping in here. They left plenty of middens behind, so they've been here a while."

"Middens?"

"Trash. Piñon and other nutshells." Jace closed the door. "I've got some supplies in my truck that I can use to patch the hole, but you may not want to use this cabinet until we get it cleaned out, patched and painted."

Alexis doubted that she would *ever* want to use it. She shuddered at the thought. "All right."

Before he headed out to his truck, Jace paused and gave her a searching look. "Are you okay? You know, living in these mountains isn't for everyone, especially for people who are accustomed to a certain level of comfort."

"In other words, it may not be for a wimp like me?" she asked, her voice testy.

He held up a hand. "Now I didn't say that. I only asked if you're okay."

"Yes." She knew her voice sounded a little too thready. "I was surprised, that's all. I assure you that I don't usually react that way. I simply don't like unpleasant surprises."

Jace's grin twitched once again. "You mean like having someone show up in the middle of the night, set fire to your yard, then announce they're staying?"

Alexis forgot about the squirrels and her embarrassment for her overreaction to them. She straightened, prepared to defend herself, but when she saw the teasing light in his eyes, she relaxed and answered, "Something like that, yes."

She offered a tentative smile, and for a moment, there was a tenuous thread of understanding between them, a friendly acceptance they hadn't known before in their short, rocky acquaintance.

It didn't last long because Jace seemed to recall what he was doing and who he was talking to. He straightened suddenly and said, "I'll see to those repairs." Quickly, he walked out and she heard the screen door close behind him.

Alexis felt a flutter of disappointment. For her, it was a pleasure to get to know someone, even someone as prickly as Jace McTaggart, on a strictly personal basis. He had no idea who she really was, or where she was from. She had the opportunity with Jace, and with the people of Sleepy River community, to prove herself as a person and as a professional. It was vitally important to her that they see her as an individual and not be influenced by any tabloidlike stories about her.

With a shrug of acceptance, Alexis returned to work. Now that the squirrels were gone, she could finish cleaning the kitchen, starting with the cupboard where the former stowaways had lived. She found a small whisk broom in a utility closet and swept out the trash they'd left, then returned to the living room to find her purse.

She pulled out a pad and pencil and began making a list of supplies she would need. Unlike most new teachers, she didn't need to pinch pennies until payday. She had plenty of money from the allowance the Inbourg national council gave her. However, she knew it wouldn't be a good idea to appear too well-off, either, in case people started asking questions about her. She would buy only what she needed immediately. She found it ironic that even here, in an area so far removed from home, she still had to be conscious of the perceptions others had of her.

As she was making her list, Alexis became aware of the sound of approaching vehicles. She glanced out the window to see Jace standing by his truck with his hands full of tools, watching as a small caravan of cars and trucks made their way into the clearing before the school and teacherage.

The vehicles stopped and women and children began pouring out. One woman, a tall, rangy redhead, called out, "Jace, Martha called to say the new teacher's here. I can't believe you let the new teacher go into that place. It's a disgrace. We were going to clean it up."

"I told her that," he answered mildly, then cocked his head toward Alexis as she came out on the porch. "She's got ideas of her own."

Alexis realized he didn't necessarily think that was a good thing, but she gave him a smile.

"We went by your place to meet Miss Chastain, but you'd already gone," the redhead continued

cheerily as she helped a little girl out of her truck.
"What in the world happened to your mailbox? And
did you have a fire?"

Alexis froze, and her gaze flew to Jace. This was
his opportunity to tell everyone how she'd arrived and
the disasters she'd caused. His dark eyes met hers
briefly, but she couldn't read his thoughts.

He gave a small shrug and answered, "Just a little
accident. We took care of it."

Alexis gave him a grateful look and he lifted an
eyebrow at her as if to ask what did she think he
would say about her? The problem was, she didn't
know. She still couldn't read him very well. Giving
up, she walked down to meet the community members who had arrived. The redhead introduced herself
as Carol Saunders, mother of two of her students, one
of whom, Billy, had a markedly wicked twinkle in his
brown eyes. Alexis instantly decided she would need
to keep a careful watch with him.

"Oh, Jace," Carol called out. "Billy returned the
quilt okay, didn't he?"

Alexis saw Jace's swift glance go from mother to
son. Billy glanced away. "Yes. I thought it was going
to stay on display at the historical society a little
longer."

"They needed that space for a display of mining
equipment, as if we haven't seen enough picks, shov-
els and miners' lamps in this county. We had to clear
out our textiles." Carol seemed to become aware of
her son's averted gaze. "Jace? There wasn't a problem with it, was there? I know how your mother treasured that quilt so I told him to ride over and bring

it to you. If I thought anything had gone wrong with it..."

"It was fine. Billy left it on the porch and we found it there." Jace's voice was smooth and reassuring but he lifted his eyes to Alexis's stricken face and she didn't feel the least bit reassured.

Carol nodded, smiled at her son, who then scampered off, and turned to Alexis with a smile. "Come meet everyone else," she invited.

One of the other women was Stella Kramer, another member of the school board who welcomed her warmly and introduced her three little girls who would be Alexis's pupils in the primary grades.

There were a couple of other families represented, but the most memorable person was an older woman, dressed in a man's oversize shirt, jeans and boots, who marched up to Alexis, handed her a quart jar of a warm golden liquid, and said, "I'm Hattie Fritz. I keep bees. That's honey. What needs doing around here?"

Alexis barely had a chance to blink and form an answer before Jace walked past on the way to repair the hole made by the squirrels. The rest of the crew took their signal from him and streamed around Alexis into the house. Within minutes, they'd dragged all the furniture and rugs outside and set the children to beating out the dust with brooms, though they were more interested in getting inside the schoolhouse and playing with the computers. However, they soon discovered that getting to beat furniture was fun, too, so they set to work. The adults then went back inside and began scrubbing every surface in sight.

Alexis quickly lost any awkwardness she felt with this good-natured bunch as she pitched in, as well. It amused her, though, to realize that, as they worked, she was very gently being grilled about what had become of Rachel Burrows and what her own qualifications were for teaching the children of the community.

Faced with this energetic group of women and children, Jace left after repairing the squirrel damage and Alexis felt guilty that she hadn't thanked him for his hospitality of the night before and his help today. He was her nearest neighbor, so she knew she would be seeing him again. Her biggest hope was that when she did, it would be under better circumstances. It wouldn't do for him to think she was in habitual need of help from her neighbors.

She smiled to herself. At home, they *had* no neighbors. The palace was in the middle of a huge estate populated by employees and their families. Alexis couldn't even imagine the shock that would erupt if she ran next door to borrow a cup of sugar from Mrs. Schroeder, the wife of the landscape architect her father had recently hired. No, she would do whatever was necessary to depend only on herself and to present herself as being completely competent and professional at every meeting she had with Jace from now on.

It wasn't long before the entire house was thoroughly clean, even the curtains hanging at the windows. When all her helpers prepared to go, Alexis thanked them profusely and watched them leave with the grateful feeling that she'd passed their inspection.

She unpacked her suitcases, wrote up her grocery list, and drove back through the mountains to buy her supplies in Morenci. While there, she went to the county seat of Clifton to register her teaching credentials with the county school superintendent's office. She held dual citizenship thanks to her American-born mother, so there was no question of her right to work in the U.S. She headed home elated that she was recognized, at least by one of the smallest counties in the state, as being qualified to teach in Sleepy River. She only hoped she could convince Jace of that.

The sound of scuffling on her porch told Alexis that someone had stopped by for a visit. The strong scent of men's cologne breezing through her house told her it was the Patchett brothers.

She had only been in her house for three days and they'd already visited four times, always together, always watching each other as if they were each afraid that one of them would find an advantage the other didn't have, causing Alexis to prefer one of them over the other. The truth was, they were nice boys, but they most certainly had romance on their minds, and she most certainly didn't.

With a sigh, she stood up from the piles of papers on her small kitchen table and went to invite them in. Impeccable manners had been drummed into her from the moment of her birth and she wouldn't even consider telling them to go away because she was busy on lesson plans for the first weeks of school.

"Evenin', Miss Chastain," Gil said as soon as he saw her. He swept his hat off his head and clapped it over his heart. "I was wondering if there was something you might need."

Rocky shuffled his brother aside. "I was wondering that, too." His unruly black hair was parted down the middle and slicked down on both sides. Alexis stared at the thick, coarse strands in amazement. Any second, she expected tufts of it to start flinging themselves skyward. She reminded herself not to get too close.

His dark eyes took on a worshipful expression. "Anything you need? Anything at all?"

Peace and quiet, Alexis thought wistfully, but she smiled softly and said, "No thank you. I'm quite all right." Instead of inviting them in, because she had learned on the night of their first visit that she would have trouble dislodging them, she opened the screen door and slipped through to stand with them on the porch.

Their faces fell so tragically that she immediately reconsidered her plan to hurry them away. She knew she was too softhearted, which was why she'd never been a good spokesperson for the Chastain family. Reporters could almost always get her to answer their questions and they'd loved her blunt answers, which was one of the reasons she'd learned to avoid them.

"Why don't you sit down for a while, though, before you head back home?" Alexis quickly sat herself in the old Adirondack chair so the two of them wouldn't try to help her into it, get in each other's way, and then into an argument.

Both boys then perched on the porch railing and looked at her expectantly. Alexis sighed inwardly, ruing the careful schooling she had received at Miss Devereaux's Academy for Young Ladies. She could converse on almost any subject and always carried the majority of any discussion with Gil and Rocky. She couldn't decide if they were always this tongue-tied around women or if they were simply dazzled by her.

She glanced down at the faded jeans and white cotton top she wore as she recalled that she had washed off her makeup and brushed her hair out of its braid when she had cleaned up after a day spent dusting and arranging shelves in the schoolhouse.

No, she didn't think they were drawn to her glamour. They simply liked being around a single woman near their own age.

She folded her hands in her lap and asked, "So please tell me what you've been doing today. I know the life of a cowboy must be very challenging. I'm sure you must need many special skills to do the job."

What the devil were they doing? At the edge of the clearing, Jace sat atop his horse, Hondo, and squinted through the twilight. For the third night in a row, Gil and Rocky had disappeared right after dinner. He'd heard them drive off in their old truck, and suspicious that they were going to visit Alexis, he'd quickly saddled Hondo. He had followed the trail of dust hanging in the still air which had turned in at the drive to the schoolhouse. Circling around to the edge of the clearing, he waited in the shadows.

Back straight, legs modestly crossed at the ankle

and drawn to one side, hands folded neatly in her lap, Alexis was sitting in that crummy old chair like a queen holding court. Gil and Rocky were seated on the railing in front of her, gazing at her much like supplicants begging for her favor.

Disgruntled, Jace glared at them. He'd hardly been able to get a lick of work out of them since she'd arrived. Having her so close by was turning out to be a major distraction. The boys, together and individually, thought of a dozen things a day they needed to do for her. Jace usually managed to head them off, but once the chores were done and dinner was over, they were on their own.

"Damned cozy scene," he muttered, spurring Hondo into an easy walk across the baseball field. He knew Alexis was busy. He'd been receiving daily bulletins from the moms who'd been over to help her. They reported back about the work she was doing, the clothes she was wearing, the full carat diamond earrings that sparkled in her ears even when she was dressed in jeans, as she was now. The women were all very impressed with her, and so was every man who had met her.

"Including me," Jace murmured. He'd spent more time thinking about her the past three days than he had about his ranch. It seemed that there was no job that could distract him from thoughts of the mysterious Alexis. He was as pitiful as Gil and Rocky, he groused to himself as he spurred Hondo forward.

When he was about ten feet away, he could hear Gil regaling Alexis with some story of a near-encounter they'd had with a wolf the previous spring.

"That's the way, boys," he said, cantering up to them. "Scare her to death."

The three of them had been so engrossed in the story that they hadn't heard them. The effect of his voice was electrifying. Gil shot to his feet and whirled around, bumping Rocky, who was precariously balanced on the porch railing. Rocky keeled over backwards, arms and legs windmilling, to sprawl in the weed-choked flower bed below.

"Yeow!" he yelped. "There's goatheads in here!" He scrambled to his feet and began picking the spiny thorns out of his backside.

"Good," Jace said unsympathetically. "What are you two doing over here, anyway, besides bothering Miss Chastain?"

"Hey," Gil defended. "We're not bothering her. We came to offer our help."

"Oh, has she run short of windy stories?"

Alexis rose to her feet to face him. "We were having a friendly chat, Mr. McTaggart."

He gave her a disgruntled look. Three days ago, when she'd run to him to escape the squirrels, she'd called him Jace. Now they were back to Mr. McTaggart. She didn't like that he'd interrupted her little rendezvous.

"Yeah, well, these guys have work to do." He nodded toward Gil. "Did you know your horse threw a shoe today?"

He saw Gil shoot Alexis a quick glance. "Of course I knew."

"Have you replaced it?"

"I'll do it in the morning, Jace."

"Okay, but tonight you'll go rub liniment on the stone bruise she got after she threw it."

Gil gave him a stormy look, as if he was ready to argue, but Alexis made a soft sound of distress. "Oh, the poor thing. Do you think she's in much pain?"

"Oh, no," Gil began, turning to her. "She'll be fine, if..." Something in her expression stopped him. He stared at her as if entranced. Jace was amazed to see that somehow, her expression conveyed the feeling that if he went and doctored that poor injured horse, she would think he was a king among men. Gil puffed out his chest. "I'll go take care of it right now. We don't want a poor, helpless creature to suffer."

Alexis beamed at him as if he'd just invented sunlight and Jace rolled his eyes. "That's good of you, Gil," she said.

Jace could see that it was a mighty effort, but Gil managed to tear his gaze away from her. "Come on, Rocky," he growled. "Let's go."

"Go? I can't even sit down. I'm still trying to get these stickers out of my butt," Rocky whined.

"Well, you stand up in the back," Jace instructed. "And I better be able to find you two when I get home. We need to have a little talk."

Both young men turned and gave him a look of dread, but Jace hardened his heart. Their father was his lifelong friend and he thought the world of their mom, but he hadn't hired them on to play nursemaid to them, or chaperone.

After the boys had roared away in their beat-up old truck, with Rocky standing in the pickup's bed, wide-legged to maintain his balance, Jace turned and looked down at Alexis.

Gazing at her, with the last rays of twilight turning that chestnut hair of hers to red-gold, and her green eyes watching him with some kind of unknowable wisdom, he could understand why the Patchetts couldn't stay away. In fact, he felt an unfamiliar catch in his gut as he looked at her.

Must be hunger, he decided abruptly. They'd had canned spaghetti for dinner and it had been far from satisfying. He was opening his mouth to tell her that he would keep the boys away when he was interrupted by the chirping of a cell phone.

"Oh."

For some reason, alarm flitted across Alexis's face. "Excuse me. I'll be right back," she said as she jumped out of the low chair and grabbed the door handle. She hurried inside, but in her haste, she didn't close the door all the way and Jace could hear her end of the conversation. A gentleman would have moved out of earshot, but the first thing Alexis said was, "Don't call me that, Esther. Here I'm only Alexis Chastain."

Eyebrows raised curiously, Jace lingered to listen.

"I'm sorry," Esther said. "I keep forgetting I'm supposed to be you."

"Please don't forget or my dad will be mad at both of us," Alexis warned and then grinned, delighted to hear Esther's familiar, grumpy voice. Though Esther was a few years older than Alexis, the two of them had been friends since childhood.

"His Highness would have a right to be angry," Esther said. "We lied to him."

Alexis winced at Esther's bluntness. "Well..."

"And if the papers find out, our goose is cooked."

Alarmed, Alexis asked, "Have they been hanging around?"

"Of course. One of them has been offering bribes to the employees for pictures of Princess Alexis."

"Oh, no."

"I'm afraid it's only a matter of time before someone accepts the offer."

She should have known it wouldn't work, Alexis thought. There were too many risks they would be found out.

"Speaking from a purely selfish standpoint, I'm not sure I'll mind," Esther went on. "Do you know what time these people get *up* around here? At five! We get out and climb rocks before breakfast. I say when you've climbed one rock, you've climbed them all. And then breakfast! Wood chips and hay."

In spite of herself, Alexis laughed. "Oh, come on, it can't be that bad. Golden Bluffs Spa is supposed to have one of the best chefs in the world."

"That's where the bluff part comes in. They trick you into coming here by putting out that story about the chef, but when you're here, he hides away and they hand out horse fodder. Personally, I plan to find out which closet they've got him in."

"Good luck, Sherlock. Seriously, it's not too bad, is it?" She and Esther would do just about anything for each other, but maybe this time she was asking too much.

"Nah," Esther sighed. "But I've lost five pounds. Never mind that I need to lose forty. I'm not used to all this activity, but I'll be all right. How are you?"

"I'm fine," Alexis began, and was about to launch into a description of Sleepy River when a horse's impatient snort reminded her she had a guest. Jace!

She whirled around and noticed for the first time that the door was partway open. Had he heard her? Frantically, she tried to recall what she had said.

Hastily, she said goodbye and hung up. Dropping the phone on the old leather sofa, she hurried back to Jace.

He still sat atop Hondo and was watching her with an unreadable expression in his eyes.

Flustered, she stammered out an apology. "I'm sorry. It was my friend, I...I'm not usually so rude." In fact, she was *never* rude.

"It's all right," Jace said, but she wasn't sure he meant it. "I only wanted to be sure the Patchetts don't bother you anymore." Saddle leather creaked as he moved. "This isn't the first time they've been over here, is it?"

Alexis hid her anxiety and walked to the edge of the porch so that they were almost at eye level. "No. They've become my most frequent visitors, along with the squirrels who keep trying to reclaim their former home. They try to run inside whenever I open the back door."

"Those little devils are pretty quick. How do you keep them out?"

She grinned. "I used to date a football player. I know some moves."

Jace chuckled. "You'll need 'em, especially if my hired hands keep hanging around." His eyes narrowed as he gazed at her. "You're a popular woman."

"It's because I'm new."

"I admit that none of us are used to strangers up here, but they shouldn't be bothering you like that," he said gruffly, pulling on Hondo's reins and tugging his head around in the direction of home. "I'll talk to them. They won't bother you again."

He rode away swiftly, leaving Alexis to gape after him in surprise.

What on earth had gotten into him? She wanted to call after him, but she didn't know what she would have said. Besides, she needed to think, to recall her conversation with Esther word for word and try to remember if she'd let anything slip.

Oh, she wasn't cut out for deception, she thought in despair. Morosely, she leaned against the porch railing and listened to Jace's horse's hooves thunder away.

An unaccustomed feeling of longing sifted through her. She wished things were different. In spite of the tension between them and his obvious belief that she was enticing Gil and Rocky away from their work, she would have liked to talk to him. He was sensible and levelheaded and she thought there were probably things he could tell her about Sleepy River community that would help her understand her students.

However, she couldn't imagine that Jace would

ever climb her front porch steps and perch on the railing, ready to settle in for a cozy visit. It was hard for her to acknowledge, but he really didn't think much of her.

Chapter Five

Never let them see you sweat. Alexis thought of that old saying as she stood before her class on the first day of school. She knew she was slightly overdressed for the occasion, in a russet-colored suit she'd bought in Paris last fall. She had wanted to look professional, though, and felt it was necessary to start the semester out on the right note.

She thought of another one she'd heard from a master teacher—*Don't smile until Thanksgiving.* She wasn't sure she could go to that extreme, but her face felt as if it was about to crack from trying to hold a friendly, yet firm, expression.

There were twelve students gazing back at her from their desks; six in primary grades and six in the intermediate grades. The younger students were looking at her as if they expected great things from her, the older students seemed to convey that they'd give her a short trial period and if she didn't work out, they would happily make her life unbearable.

Billy Saunders appeared to be eyeing her with speculation, ready to see exactly how far he could push her.

Alexis took a deep breath and plunged in, greeting the students, telling them what she expected of them, and establishing the rules of the class. Before she was a third of the way through her little speech, Billy's hand shot into the air.

"Yes, Billy."

"What if we don't agree with your classroom rules?" he asked, glancing around to make sure everyone was listening.

Round one, Alexis thought. She folded her hands at her waist. "Some rules are negotiable and some aren't. Good behavior and good manners aren't negotiable."

He slumped in his chair and stuck his feet out before him. "What about homework? I have a lot of chores when I get home so I can't do homework."

Alexis thought fleetingly of Jace's comment about the chores he'd been expected to do after the long ride home on the bus. She suspected that, even then, he'd managed to get his assignments done. "Homework is anything you don't finish in class so I suggest you stay on task and get your work done as accurately and quickly as possible. If it appears that you can't do both chores at home and your classroom assignments, I'll call your parents in for a conference and we'll solve the problem together."

He stared at her for a second. Having his parents

come to school wasn't an idea he relished. "Never mind," he muttered.

Even though she knew she'd only delayed a confrontation between them, Alexis nodded and went on.

The rest of the day went smoothly, much to Alexis's relief and pleasure, even though the younger children needed a great deal of her time and attention. Whenever she turned her back on Billy, she suspected he was up to mischief. He appeared to be hiding something in his desk and she knew she would have to deal with it before the end of the day, but the time slipped by and she was too busy to stop and take him aside.

When she released school for the day, the children rushed out to their parents' cars, she spoke to several people and waved them off. When they were gone, she leaned against the doorjamb and allowed her shoulders to slump with weariness, then massaged the back of her neck to ease the tension there. After a moment, she took a deep breath, straightened, and went back inside to collapse in her desk chair and stare at the empty room. Now she knew why someone had once described teaching elementary school as "trying to back a thirty-car train down a mountainside in a blizzard with no brakes." Being in front of an audience and thinking on her feet constantly for seven hours was exhausting.

In the stand of pine trees at the edge of the baseball field, Jace leaned forward to quiet Hondo, speaking easily even as his eyes stayed glued to the door of the school.

He should leave, he knew. He'd only come by to see how things had gone, then lingered out of sight so he could gauge the children's reactions as they departed. Not that he was sure what he'd been looking for—maybe little girls running to their mothers, crying hysterically that Miss Chastain was the meanest teacher ever and they didn't want to go back to school.

He knew better than that, but Alexis had been on his mind all day, even while he'd been wrestling with his hated paperwork. He'd decided to take a break and ride over to see how the first day had gone.

What he had seen had surprised him; Alexis dressed in a suit the likes of which the White Mountains had never seen, the children giving her hugs as they'd left. They'd seemed happy, he'd satisfied his curiosity, and he really ought to leave.

But he didn't. He had seen the way she had slumped in the doorway with exhaustion when everyone was gone.

She looked so frail and tired that Jace was blindsided by a surge of protectiveness for her.

For the first time, he thought about what it must have cost her to leave her family—wherever they were—and move here to teach. She had been eager enough for the assignment, but now he wondered if she regretted it.

A life-insurance policy was included in her benefits and he'd taken a peek at the beneficiary, which turned out to be the Chastain family trust account, which told him exactly nothing. Her next of kin was listed as her father, Michael Chastain, who had an out-of-the-country phone number and a post office box in Paris. There was no indication that she wasn't an American citizen. She certainly didn't have a green card to work in the United States, so she had to be a citizen. She never spoke of her family, though. It made him think her relationship with her family was as strained as his had been with his father before the unbending old man had died.

Jace shifted uncomfortably in the saddle. He didn't want to think of her as a woman with a family, with problems, with needs. He simply wanted her to be the schoolteacher, to handle all the problems at the school so he wouldn't have to. Nothing more.

Alexis was too tired to do more than catch her breath for a few minutes. This was far different from student teaching where she'd had a class of third-graders whose ability levels were all about the same. These children ranged from two beginning readers to one who read at high school level.

For the first time, Alexis began to feel doubtful about her ability to handle the class and she wished she had someone to talk to. A mentor would be very helpful. Of course, she could talk to Martha Singleton and ask her advice, but Martha had two children in the school and Alexis was afraid her questions could worry Martha, who then might report to the school board, and most especially to Jace, that Alexis couldn't do the job.

No, she thought, flexing her feet inside her shoes as she longed to go to her little house and change into jeans and sneakers. She would continue to do her best, and if she needed help, she would call some teachers she knew in Phoenix and ask their advice.

Besides, she hadn't seen Jace since the day he had rounded up Gil and Rocky and sent them scurrying home and she'd just as soon leave it that way.

A faint rustling noise broke the stillness of the deserted classroom. Recalling the squirrels in the kitchen cupboard, Alexis stood and listened. The sound seemed to be coming from Billy's desk and she recalled the interest and activity that had surrounded him all afternoon.

Cautiously, she approached and leaned down to peer inside the open front of the desk. A triangular-shaped head with two small eyes stared back at her. It took a few seconds for her to realize she was looking at a snake.

"Oh!" she yelped in surprise, straightened and backed away, hand to her throat. She and the reptile regarded each other warily.

"Darn that boy," she gasped. He must have caught the snake when he and the others were outside at lunchtime, then gone off and left it. Maybe he couldn't figure out a way to sneak it into his backpack and get it home.

Distressed, Alexis rubbed the back of her hand across her lips. She had no experience in dealing with snakes. Too bad Mr. Schroeder, the palace landscape architect, or even her nephew Jean Louis, weren't here. They would have known what to do.

After a moment's thought, she approached the desk and grasped it by the back. Lifting it and moving swiftly, she tilted it so that everything inside slid to the back, praying all the while that the snake wouldn't leap out and that it wasn't poisonous if it did.

Hurtling herself and the desk toward the door, she yelled again when the snake popped its head out as she thumped the desk down on the porch floor. Staggering slightly, she dragged the desk out and heaved it into the grass.

Everything in the desk flew out, including the snake which arced through the air and into the bushes. Alexis took a relieved breath that the creature was gone, but she didn't have time to relax because hoofbeats thundering across the field had her looking up to see Jace racing toward her.

He was in front of her, reining Hondo to a halt before she could think to step back.

"What in the world are you doing?" he demanded, staring down at her. "Do you always end the first day of school by throwing the desks outside? Were the kids that hard on you?"

Alexis blinked up at him. He looked formidable, seated on his horse which was at least seventeen hands high, his midnight-dark eyes glaring at her from beneath the brim of his cowboy hat.

"No, certainly...certainly not," she floundered. "The children were fine. You don't need to..." She paused and frowned up at him as she realized why he had arrived so quickly. "Were you spying on me?" she asked, placing her hands on her hips. "I don't think your duties as head of the school board stretch quite that far." She had been secretly watched enough times in her life that she didn't react to it well now.

His gaze flickered. "I had business over this way,

and besides, you're hardly the one to be questioning me when you're tossing desks outside. What happened?''

Her mouth tightened. She was reluctant to answer him, but she finally lifted her chin and said, ''I was simply dealing with a snake that was in one of the desks.''

''A snake?'' He reached up and pushed his hat back with his thumb. ''How'd a snake get inside?''

''One of the children put it there,'' she answered in a cool tone. ''But I assure you it's not a problem.'' She gestured to the overturned desk. ''As you can see, I've dealt with it.''

''And how,'' he murmured. ''Who's desk is that?''

Alexis lifted her hands. ''I'd rather not say. It's a discipline problem that I can certainly deal with on my own tomorrow, and...''

''By throwing the kid out along with his desk?'' Jace asked, dismounting. He picked it up and set it back on the porch, then began gathering up the books and supplies.

''No!'' She hurried over to stop him.

Jace paused, gazing down at a spiral notebook that had a king cobra on the cover. ''It was Billy Saunders, wasn't it?''

Alexis searched his face. ''How did you know?''

''The kid loves snakes. Took one to church one Sunday a few months ago. Caused quite a stir.''

''I can imagine.''

Jace mounted the steps to the schoolroom easily, carrying the desk and all its contents. Inside the door, he asked, ''Where do you want this?''

Alexis hurried ahead of him, indicating Billy's place.

Jace thumped it into its spot and turned to her. "As I see it, you can handle this one of two ways."

Here we go again, she thought, her temper rising. "I don't need your advice on handling Billy," she said, though she knew she was being unnecessarily testy. "And, frankly, I don't think it's your job as head of the school board to give me advice on teaching or on discipline."

He ignored her, which annoyed her even further. Instead, he frowned at her and said, "You see, his mom doesn't want snakes in the house, so he can't have them there. What you need to do is have your own herpetorium and put him in charge."

Alexis repressed a shudder. "A herpetorium? A snake house?"

"Yeah, make him the ultimate authority on snakes in the classroom. I guarantee you, you'll have less trouble with him."

If she took away all his privileges in school, she would probably have less trouble with him, as well, she thought stubbornly, but then she calmed a little. No, she would have even *more* trouble with him.

"I'll take your suggestion under advisement," she responded in a tone similar to one her father used when he was reluctant to take advice from his know-it-all first secretary.

His frown changed to an amused look. "You do that. And here's something else you should think about."

Alexis squared her shoulders and faced him, chin in the air. "And what, exactly, would that be?"

"You know, when you give me that look, I get the feeling you should be wearing a diamond tiara and handing down royal edicts from a throne."

Alexis started visibly and she felt the color washing out of her face. "What...what do you mean?"

Jace's dark eyes narrowed and he stepped forward. "Hey, I didn't mean to upset you," he said, his voice gruff. "I just meant that you can give a very cold look when you want to."

Relief relaxed her muscles. "It's something teachers learn quickly. Now what other piece of advice did you have for me?" She tried to keep her tone of voice from sounding as though she wouldn't take his advice no matter what it was, but wasn't sure she succeeded.

Jace stared at her for a few seconds before answering. "That suit," he said, indicating her designer original. "It looks nice, but jeans would do just as well."

Alexis almost laughed at the idea of a Charles Piccard original being described as "nice." "I wanted to look professional."

"And uncompromising," he murmured, giving it another glance.

Alexis had been quite pleased with the way she'd held onto her temper, but now, she could feel it simmering. "It's important to dress in a professional manner. It gives people confidence that you know what you're doing," she informed him in what she knew was a pedantic tone. "When you get together with others in your profession, don't you dress up?"

This time he laughed out loud. "No, jeans and boots pretty much do it for me and the rest of the ranchers. We don't spend a lot of thought on clothes since we're busy worrying about range management, feeding cattle, and now about keeping our herds moving to avoid the wolves that have been reintroduced to this area."

Alexis felt embarrassment tinged with regret. She had been so busy preparing for school and focusing on what she needed to do, that she hadn't given much thought to the problems and challenges of being a rancher in this area. Somehow, it only served to point up the vast gulf between herself and Jace. It made her feel sad, which was confusing in itself since she hardly knew this man. She reached up and pushed back strands of the chestnut hair that had pulled out of her French twist when she had been tussling with the desk.

"No," she said quietly. "Of course not. Well, um, thank you for stopping by, but I assure you, I have everything under control now that I've evicted Billy's snake, and I'll think about your suggestion to put him in charge of a classroom snake project, and...believe me, I know how to dress appropriately."

"Well good." Jace turned away and headed for the door, then hesitated. "There's one more thing." He paused and an uncomfortable look passed over his face.

"What?" She braced herself for more corrections of her behavior, dress, actions.

Jace reached up and rubbed the back of his hand across his jaw. "I've managed to keep Gil and Rocky from pestering you for nine days now, but I don't think I can hold them off much longer.''

"Oh?"

"So, I'm thinking maybe you should come over for dinner.''

"You invited her to dinner?" Gil asked, staring at Jace.

"You really did?" The expression on Rocky's face was that of someone who had come downstairs on Christmas morning to find Santa Claus parking a sleek sports car in the living room.

"Yes, I really did." Jace gazed at them, uneasy at confirming the thought that he'd made a terrible mistake. When he'd promised their parents that he would watch out for them as well as pay them fairly, he'd had no idea that he would have to deal with their megadose of puppy love for the new schoolteacher.

He'd issued his invitation to her on Monday and it was now Friday. He'd had a full week to fluctuate between anticipation and regret. He hadn't told Gil and Rocky until today because they would have driven him absolutely insane over the whole thing.

Gil and Rocky looked at each other. "Why?" Gil asked. "You've been threatening to horsewhip us if we even *thought* about going over to offer her our help.''

Jace winced, recalling that threat, but he'd felt justified when he'd found the two brothers visiting Alexis.

"She seemed to have plenty of help," he said evasively. In truth, he hadn't known how much help she had, or needed. The women of the community had taken over for him, and he'd been glad to let them, though he actually heard frequent reports, mostly about her fabulous clothes. "But we're her nearest neighbors and even though she'll only be here a few months, we should get to know her."

The Patchetts gaped at him.

Jace, who hadn't blushed since he'd gone through puberty, could feel his face turning red at that blatantly lame excuse. Gil and Rocky seemed willing to swallow it, though, if it meant getting them closer to the goddess they adored.

The boys grinned, then Rocky's face fell. "Does that mean we have to cook?"

"I'll cook," Jace growled, feeling more ridiculous by the moment.

"But you only know how to cook eggs, bacon and steak, and she's already had your eggs and bacon," Gil pointed out.

"Then I'll cook steak," Jace said, exasperated. He pointed at Gil. "You can bake some potatoes. Anybody ought to be able to do that."

"Even you," Rocky said, grinning as he began edging from the room.

"And you." Jace pinned Rocky with his pointing finger. "You can make a salad and…and some salad dressing."

Rocky's mouth sagged. "Are you kidding? I don't know how to make salad dressing."

"Then call your mom and ask her." Feeling more ridiculous by the moment, Jace swung away. "I'm going to take a shower and change clothes."

There was a moment of silence behind him as it seemed to occur to Gil and Rocky that they had to do that, as well. In fact, this was the moment they'd been breathlessly anticipating since Jace had forbidden them to bother Alexis, though they each would have preferred to be alone with her.

The thundering of boots had Jace diving to one side, grabbing the stair rail, and almost flipping over it as the boys barreled past him to beat each other to the shower. Shoving and shouting, they thundered their way upstairs.

Jace shook his head as he went into his own room. Fortunately, his bathroom had its own water heater because there would be none left after Gil and Rocky finished.

He pulled clean, but wrinkled, underwear from a drawer where he'd thrown it after removing it from the dryer a few days ago. He and his hired hands didn't worry much about folding their clothes away neatly as their mothers had taught them. Clean they needed, folded didn't matter.

Jace walked to his closet and threw open the door. *He'd invited her for dinner.* Jace considered that thought as he stared dumbfoundedly at the shirts hanging in the closet. He saw work shirts, a few dressy white ones, including one that actually didn't look too bad if you didn't notice the place where he'd inexpertly sewn on a button after getting the cuff caught on a fence post last spring. And he was almost certain he had some fairly new jeans in here somewhere.

What he'd told Alexis was true, that jeans and

boots pretty much covered his wardrobe needs, but then he rarely went anywhere other than local towns where he bought supplies—and he only did that when he couldn't convince Gil and Rocky to go in his place. His friends and neighbors teased him about it, but Jace was a confirmed stay-at-home. Jace loved his ranch and rarely thought it was necessary to leave it.

In spite of the rough way he'd been raised—by a demanding father willing to sacrifice everything to the needs of the Running M, including his wife—Jace loved the ranch. The one woman with whom he'd ever been seriously involved said it was his *only* love, and he couldn't deny it.

Jace frowned, not sure why he was thinking about things like that when he was supposed to be getting dressed. He searched through the articles hanging in the closet until he found the nearly new jeans near the back. He pulled them out, brushed off the line of dust that topped the crease left by the hanger, and tossed them on the bed.

If he would face up to the truth, he would admit that he didn't know the first thing about having a woman over for dinner. He didn't date. The few women available in Sleepy River were married and trips into town for female companionship took up too much time. That's why he'd long since reconciled himself to being single.

Which brought him back to thinking about why he'd invited Alexis to dinner. To *dinner?*

In spite of what he'd told the boys, he wasn't sure exactly why he'd done it. Alexis had looked tired at the end of her first day of school and he'd felt a tug of sympathy for her. He knew what it was like to have worked hard and not been sure there was any reward for it.

He'd been alarmed, and then touched, at the way she'd dragged Billy's desk outside and heaved it into the grass to get rid of the snake. She'd seemed determined to handle it on her own and he'd admired that even as he'd shaken his head in wonder at the clothes she'd been wearing. A fancy suit and high heels weren't anything he'd ever seen on a Sleepy River schoolteacher before. Martha almost always wore slacks or jeans, especially when it got cold outside.

As he showered and changed, Jace couldn't stop thinking about Alexis and he finally concluded it was because he still wasn't sure he'd done the right thing in allowing her to stay. He hadn't heard anything negative about her from any of the students' mothers, but they were women who were busy running their ranches and their families, so maybe they hadn't had time to stop and concentrate on the job Alexis was doing. Time enough for that when the newness of the first weeks of school wore off.

Somehow, that seemed to point up the differences between her and the local women. They were strong, hardy wives and mothers who were at ease baking bread or branding cattle. For all her determination, he suspected that Alexis would turn green at the sound of bawling calves and the stench of scorched hair that filled the air at branding time.

Jace paused with his razor halfway to his face and stared at his lathered-up reflection in the mirror. What did it matter if she turned green at branding time? She wouldn't even *be* here at branding time.

He lifted his razor and took a swipe at his beard. He needed to stop fantasizing. Gil and Rocky did enough of that for everyone.

Alexis slowly climbed the steps to Jace's front porch, recalling her first night in Sleepy River and the way she'd set fire to his grass. She was relieved to see that it was growing back and the evidence of her clumsiness would soon be covered by fresh growth. She still didn't know what she was going to do about the ruined quilt. He had spurned her offers to pay for it, but for someone like her, whose home was filled with antiques and treasured heirlooms hundreds of years old, it was torture to know she had ruined something of such sentimental value. She wouldn't give up her attempts to replace the quilt. It was only a matter of catching him in the right mood.

Nervously, she ran her hands down the front of her skirt, a long broomstick one in patterns of turquoise and peach, which she had paired with a peach-colored silk blouse. She had dithered for half an hour over what to wear, ironically aware that she hadn't been so anxious since her introduction to the King and Queen of Spain. In fact, she didn't think she had been this nervous even then.

She knew it stemmed from her desire to fit in and the certain knowledge that she wasn't doing so. For the most part, her students were well-behaved and their parents were polite, but they viewed her with puzzlement as if she was some kind of tropical bird that had landed in these mountains. It distressed her, but she didn't quite know how to solve it. Nothing in her life had prepared her for this and she couldn't recall anything from her classes that had mentioned how to become part of a community. That's why she had accepted Jace's invitation. In spite of the smallness of the community, he was almost the only person she knew in Sleepy River and she hoped to be able to ask him for suggestions on what she should do.

Deep in thought, Alexis started when Jace's voice roared from inside the house. "If you two yahoos don't quit fighting over the mirror, I'm going to break it over your heads."

Alexis paused with her fist an inch from the door. "Okay," she murmured. "Maybe he's not in the right mood tonight to give me advice." The sound of his voice had kicked her heartbeat up several notches. Odd that his anger didn't frighten her. She found it exhilarating, something like skiing straight down a mountain and landing face-first in a snowdrift.

She knocked and then jumped back when she heard a stampede toward the door. The door was swept open by Gil, no, by Rocky, no, by Gil who was showered, shampooed, and shined up to within an inch of his life. He grabbed the door by its frame, elbowed his brother out of the way, and then blocked him, all the while grinning at Alexis with a dopey expression.

Eyes wide, she stared at the two tussling young men, but before she could say anything, Jace intervened, grabbing each of them by an arm and hauling them out of the way. "Don't mind them," he instructed her. "Their parents are normal, but insanity has obviously struck in this generation."

The boys didn't seem offended by Jace's manhandling. They grinned happily at her and Gil said, "Why don't you come on in? Can I take your coat?"

"Why'd you say that?" Rocky asked frowning at his brother, giving him a backhanded slap across the bicep. "I was going to say that. Mom always said we were supposed to offer to take a lady's coat," he explained to Alexis who answered with a weak smile.

"She's not *wearing* a coat," Jace roared, reaching out and touching the fluttery, lettuce-hemmed edge of her blouse. "It's seventy-five degrees outside. Why the devil would she need a coat?"

"Oh, yeah," Rocky said. "Why didn't you notice that, Gil?"

Alexis could feel laughter bubbling inside. She hoped she could keep it under control through what promised to be a long evening. "Something smells wonderful," she said, edging closer to Jace, who seemed like the only safe haven in the place.

"Baked potatoes," Gil said puffing out his chest. "I made 'em. My secret recipe."

Beside her, she could hear Jace snorting derisively. "Baked potatoes don't need a recipe. You just bake them, and... Oh, never mind," he grumbled.

Alexis couldn't resist a look at his face. He had the appearance of a man who was wondering how he'd gotten himself caught in a whirlpool as he went down for the third time. She gave him a secret grin that said she knew the two of them needed to stick together this evening. Jace answered with an apologetic little shrug, admitting he'd probably made a mistake, but the two of them could soldier on together.

"And I made salad," Rocky added, not to be outdone by his bragging brother. With the strategic use of an elbow and a foot, he managed to edge past both Jace and Gil to stand close to Alexis. "And dressing to go with it. I got the recipe from a book."

The four of them were now standing in a space of about eight square feet, not enough for an average-sized woman and three cowboys. Alexis stepped back, but the two younger men advanced.

"Oh yeah? Who read it to you?" Gil asked.

"Hey," Rocky protested, giving Alexis an embarrassed sideways glance. "Quit acting like a jerk."

"Both of you quit acting like jerks," Jace said. Taking Alexis's arm, he brought her protectively close to his side and said. "If you two don't settle down, I'm going to gather up all the food and take it over to Alexis's house and she and I will eat it there."

The brothers didn't seem to hear him. Instead, they took another step closer to each other, jaws stuck out, eyes narrowed. Rocky raised his hand as if to shove his brother on the shoulder, but he never got the chance because Jace lifted his arm to stop him. Alexis, who had leaned forward just at that moment, got Jace's elbow full in the eye.

Chapter Six

"Ouch!" Alexis's hand flew up protectively as the world went momentarily black from the blow.

"Oh my God." Jace's voice was horrified as he reached for her, his arm going around her waist, and leaning her against him. "I'm sorry, Alexis, I..."

After the first intense moment of pain subsided, she shook her head. "It's all right."

"You hit her," Gil said, scandalized. "You hit a woman."

"Yeah, Jace." Rocky echoed his brother's out-raged tone. "Why'd you hit her?"

Alexis could hear Jace's growl rumble against her ear as he said, "Oh for God's sake, I didn't do it on purpose. As usual, I was getting between you two. Rocky, open the door."

Though her injured eye was watering badly, Alexis could see well enough to know that they were at last going inside the house. Jace's touch on her was gentle and protective as he compelled her into the entryway and then into the living room. Sitting her down in a chair, he snapped on a lamp and turned her face toward it, emitting a low hiss of dismay at what he saw.

"What?" she asked, alarmed. "How bad is it?"

"Not good," he said, his face full of regret. "I've got a darned hard elbow. I didn't think I hit you that hard, but this is already puffing and turning dark."

"I bruise easily," she answered, holding up her arm to indicate the pale skin on the inside of her wrist. "I'm thin-skinned."

His lips quirked and his gaze met hers. "I'm sorry about that because you're going to have a black eye."

"No," she cried. "No, I can't. I'm…" Through her mind rushed thoughts and scenarios of what people would think. She could visualize the tabloid headlines: Princess Alexis In Brawl At Wild Night Spot— Black Eye Is Result—Inbourg Royal Family Humiliated.

Immediately, she felt a surge of relief as she realized that wouldn't happen. In spite of Esther's dire prediction, the tabloids didn't know where she was, but the questions from her students would be no less curious. She could only imagine what kind of spin the imaginative Billy Saunders would put on it in front of the students whose respect she was trying to gain.

"It'll heal in a few days," Jace assured her, but she gave him a baleful look. He had the grace to appear embarrassed. "I'll get something to put on it." He stepped back and nearly tripped over Gil and

Rocky who were hovering at his heels. "Will you two get out of my way?" he roared. "Go finish getting dinner ready."

His tone of voice brooked no disobedience and the two young men scurried off with apologetic looks in Alexis's direction.

"Jace?" she asked.

"Yes?"

"Could you bring me a mirror, please?"

He frowned. "I don't think you want to see it."

"Oh, yes I do. I need to know the worst."

He hesitated for a moment longer, then he nodded and said, "Okay, but don't say I didn't warn you."

As three pairs of boots thumped their way across the wooden floor, Alexis lay back and closed her eyes.

Tears welled beneath her lids, especially the puffy one. She was so tired that all she'd wanted to do was rest this weekend and prepare for next week. Now she had to nurse a black eye. She sighed. If she wasn't careful, she would soon be indulging in self-pity, an absolute no-no in the eyes of the two New England women who had raised her—her mother and her nanny.

Jace was back in a couple of minutes with a shaving mirror. He handed it to her and she surveyed the damage. Sure enough, the area around her eye was puffy and discolored.

She moaned. "It looks just like it did that time I got caught between the paparazzi and a bodyguard. For two weeks, I had to stay out of sight inside

PLAY "LUCKY 7" AND GET
THREE FREE GIFTS!

HOW TO PLAY:

1. With a coin, carefully scratch off the silver box at the right. Then check the claim chart see what we have for you — **2 FREE BOOKS** and a gift — **ALL YOURS! ALL FREE!**

2. Send back this card and you'll receive two brand-new Silhouette Romance® novels. The books have a cover price of $3.50 each in the U.S. and $3.99 each in Canada, but they a yours to keep absolutely free.

3. There's no catch. You're under obligation to buy anything. W charge nothing — ZERO — f your first shipment. And you dor have to make any minimum numb of purchases — not even one!

4. The fact is thousands of readers enjoy receiving their books by mail from the Silhoue Reader Service.™ They enjoy the convenience of home delivery…they like getting the be new novels at discount prices, BEFORE they're available in stores…and they love their *He to Heart* newsletter featuring author news, horoscopes, recipes, book reviews and much mor

5. We hope that after receiving your free books you'll want to remain a subscriber. B the choice is yours — to continue or cancel, any time at all! So why not take us up on o invitation, with no risk of any kind. You'll be glad you did!

YOURS FREE!

PLAY LUCKY 7 FOR THIS EXCITING FREE GIFT!

THIS SURPRISE MYSTERY GIFT COULD BE YOURS FREE WHEN YOU PLAY

LUCKY 7!

Visit us online at
www.eHarlequin.com

PLAY THE

LUCKY 7

SLOT MACHINE GAME!

Just scratch off the silver box with a coin. Then check below to see the gifts you get!

YES!

I have scratched off the silver box. Please send me the 2 FREE books and gift for which I qualify. I understand I am under no obligation to purchase any books, as explained on the back and opposite page.

315 SDL C6M9

215 SDL C6M4
(S-R-OS-01/01)

| | | |
NAME (PLEASE PRINT CLEARLY)

| | | |
ADDRESS

| | | |
APT.#   CITY

STATE/PROV.   ZIP/POSTAL CODE

7	7	7	WORTH TWO FREE BOOKS PLUS A BONUS MYSTERY GIFT!
🍒	🍒	🍒	WORTH TWO FREE BOOKS!
♣	♣	♣	WORTH ONE FREE BOOK!
🔔	🔔	🍒	TRY AGAIN!

The Silhouette Reader Service™ — Here's how it works:

Accepting your 2 free books and gift places you under no obligation to buy anything. You may keep the books and gift and return the shipping statement marked "cancel." If you do not cancel, about a month later we'll send you 6 additional novels and bill you just $2.90 each in the U.S., or $3.25 each in Canada, plus 25¢ shipping & handling per book and applicable taxes if any.* That's the complete price and — compared to cover prices of $3.50 each in the U.S. and $3.99 each in Canada — it's quite a bargain! You may cancel at any time, but if you choose to continue, every month we'll send you 6 more books, which you may either purchase at the discount price or return to us and cancel your subscription.

*Terms and prices subject to change without notice. Sales tax applicable in N.Y. Canadian residents will be charged applicable provincial taxes and GST.

BUSINESS REPLY MAIL

FIRST-CLASS MAIL   PERMIT NO. 717   BUFFALO, NY

POSTAGE WILL BE PAID BY ADDRESSEE

SILHOUETTE READER SERVICE
3010 WALDEN AVE
PO BOX 1867
BUFFALO NY 14240-9952

NO POSTAGE
NECESSARY
IF MAILED
IN THE
UNITED STATES

the…'' Abruptly, she realized what she'd been saying and she clamped her mouth shut.

"Paparazzi?" Jace asked. "Bodyguard?"

Her mouth dry, she stared at him through her one good eye. Why did she let her mind wander like that? "It was…a long time ago, I…" Her words stopped. She couldn't say anything else without going into lengthy explanations, and she wasn't ready to do that quite yet.

Jace crouched before her, resting easily on the toes of his boots as he would have done if he was tending a campfire. His hands clasped his thighs and he was very still as his gaze searched her face. He looked as if he wanted to say something to her, but he seemed to glimpse her stricken face and puffy eye and thought better of it.

His voice was low and mortally serious as he said, "Someday soon, Alexis, you need to give me some answers."

Fear pummeled at her heart. Oh, she really didn't want to answer those questions. So far she had told only enough about herself and her family to get by. She refused to lie—she was terrible at it, anyway, so it would be pointless for her to try it. Her guilt over the half truth she'd told her father was torturing her.

She was also terrible at bluffing because her fair skin always blushed bright red, but she attempted it. "I'm…I'm sure you know everything you need to about me," she stammered. Color washed into her cheeks.

"Like hell," he muttered, and surged to his feet

abruptly. He took a couple of prowling turns around the room.

She tried to think of something to say to change the subject, but at that moment, Gil scurried up with a plate in his hand. "Here you go, Jace," he said breathlessly, then gaped at Alexis, his eyes bulging. "Holy cow, that's a beaut! What kind of story are you going to tell the kids at school about it? That you got in a fight? That Jace hit you? Maybe it'd be better if you just told 'em you were in a bar fight, that way, with all those fists flying and everything, you wouldn't have to be real specific about who it was that hit you. They wouldn't have to know it was Jace, the head of the school board. They all respect him and they don't need to know that he's the kind who'd hit a..."

"*Will you shut up?*" Jace bellowed. He grabbed the plate. Gil, finally realizing how furious his boss was, stumbled backwards, staring at him. His Adam's apple bobbed as he swallowed.

"Uh, yeah, sure, Jace. I'll just..." He turned and loped toward the kitchen.

Alexis gulped back laughter at the way Jace had sent his hired man packing.

Muttering about "boneheaded idiots," Jace moved to sit beside her on the sofa. From the plate Gil had brought him, he lifted a raw steak and held it up. "This is the advantage to living on a ranch—plenty of raw steak for black eyes."

Alexis stared at the bloody thing. She wasn't particularly squeamish, but she couldn't imagine having it touch her skin. "You're kidding."

He shrugged. "Sorry, but it's the best treatment. I learned it from my dad."

She gulped and asked faintly, "Oh, did he have a lot of black eyes?"

Jace raised one of his thick eyebrows at her. "Oh, I see. It's okay for you to ask questions about my family, but I can't ask about yours?"

Alexis met his curious gaze and couldn't think of a thing to say. Wordlessly, she reached out, took the steak, and placed it over her eye as she tilted her head to rest against the back of the sofa. The chill of it actually felt good on her skin and she settled back, hoping it would perform a miracle.

"I don't suppose there's any chance this will work some kind of magic and completely heal my eye before eight o'clock on Monday morning, is there?"

"Worried about facing your students?" Jace sat carefully back against the cushions so as not to jar her. His arm rested along its high back. Alexis gave him a faintly surprised look. It was the most relaxed pose she'd ever seen him in.

"A little." She was unwilling to reveal the depths of her distress to him, but she knew it seeped through in her voice.

"Don't listen to Gil. Just tell the kids it was an accident. Living on cattle ranches as they do, they know all about accidents."

"I suppose you're right," she said slowly, touched by his matter-of-fact approach. "But it still looks awful."

"Don't worry about appearances, Alexis," he said gruffly. "You've got substance."

Turning, she blinked at him through her uninjured eye. Tears welled suddenly and tumbled down her cheek. "That's the nicest thing you've ever said to me."

"Well if saying nice things makes you cry, I guess it's a good thing I'm such a grouch." Jace lifted his hips and reached into his back pocket for a clean handkerchief. He took her trembling chin in his hand and gave her face a firm swipe, taking a moment to tidy up the area around the seeping steak, as well.

"Tha...ank you," she hiccuped.

Jace plucked the raw meat away and gave her eye a careful examination. In spite of her pain and embarrassment, Alexis was impressed by the gentleness of his touch.

She was relieved to discover that the swelling around her injured eye did seem to be receding a little bit, enough for her to be able to look at Jace. As she had the morning after they had met, she admired the strength of his face, offset by his incongruously soft lashes. A sharp pang of longing seared her and she gasped softly.

Jace looked up. "Did I hurt you?"

She gave a slight shake of her head because she couldn't speak. A faint panic fluttered in her throat. This man was so attractive, so vital that she felt confused and frightened even as she was drawn to him.

Jace McTaggart was nothing like the men her father thought would be suitable for her. Prince Michael had investigated three businessmen and an earl as potential husbands for her because he said they were "real men," the kind who would take care of her and give her a comfortable life.

How wrong he was. A real man was one who let a woman take care of herself if that was her choice, one who shunned a comfortable life for a satisfying one.

As he looked at her, Jace's eyes seemed to lighten and soften. A slight smile curved one corner of his mouth. It fascinated her to see him do that. "Alexis," he said softly. "What are you thinking?"

"I'm thinking about what kind of man you are," she whispered.

Surprise flickered in his eyes. "Why would you be doing that?"

She smiled at his skeptical tone. "Because I recently received a blow to the head."

His lips quirked. "What kind of man am I?"

"I...I think you're hard."

"I won't deny that."

"And honest."

"I hope so. Anything else?"

She swallowed. "I'm thinking that you like your life here and would never want to leave."

His eyes narrowed thoughtfully. "That's right. My life is here."

She had no idea where these thoughts and questions were coming from, but she went on. "Is that why you're not married? Before you hired Gil and Rocky, did you rattle around all by yourself in this place that's big enough for a family of ten? And did you like it that way?"

He blinked, taken aback by her questions. "Alexis..."

"Because I know what it's like to live in a big place and to be lonely...."

"Do you, Alexis? I'm sorry." His hand lifted to touch her cheek. This time, he wasn't interested in wiping her tears. Lightly, he ran his index finger along her velvety skin. "Being lonely is hell. Have you been lonely since you came to Sleepy River?"

"Not really because I've been busy, and..." She looked into his steady, dark eyes. "Some," she admitted. "And it's much quieter here than it is in...than what I'm used to."

"Don't visits from Gil and Rocky liven things up?"

Alexis shook her head. "Not enough."

The arm Jace had stretched along the back of the couch came around to rest lightly on her shoulder and draw her nearer to him. His lips quirked in a little smile and his eyes softened with humor. "I'm sorry. I didn't mean to deprive you of their company, but I thought they were probably distracting you from your work."

Alexis laughed softly. "They were."

"It seems that even when I try, I can't quite do what's right for you."

Alexis tilted her head. "Why would you need to?"

"An overdeveloped sense of responsibility, I suppose," he answered in an ironic tone.

Alexis looked into his eyes and it struck her suddenly that she really had no idea how old he was. She would have said he was in his mid to late thirties, but now she wondered. He actually looked somewhat younger than that. It was the weight of responsibility that he carried that had formed those lines around his eyes. For some reason, she thought about her father, carrying the responsibility for his small principality, and of her grandfather, burying the country's precious keepsakes with his own hands so that the Nazis couldn't torture their whereabouts out of an innocent farmer.

These men had spent their lives keeping everyone's well-being in mind, striving to make sure everyone had everything they needed. It was exactly as Jace dealt with his diverse neighbors—even to having a couple of court jesters in the form of Gil and Rocky.

"Yes," she answered quietly. "I can see that. I never realized…"

"What?" he asked when she paused.

"How much owning and operating a ranch could be like running your own kingdom."

He chuckled. "Kingdom? Not with the county, state and federal governments breathing down my neck."

A spasm of consternation crossed her face. "They give you a lot of trouble, do they? That's another thing I didn't know."

"No more trouble than they give any other rancher. It's only that they each have their own agenda, and often they don't correspond."

She frowned. "It would make more sense if they did."

This time he laughed, a deep, rich sound that sent unexpected ripples of pleasure up her spine. "Honey, it's government. It doesn't *have* to make sense." He tilted his head. "Oh, I forgot, your family is in some kind of government work, isn't it?"

Heat flooded her face. Uh-oh. She would have to be careful of what she said. "That's right."

"What, exactly?"

"I'm...not at liberty to say," she hedged. Oh, how she wished he would drop this. She didn't want to lie to him, but she had begun her job here on her own terms. Even at that, he seemed to have had a hard enough time accepting her. He was such a straightforward man, she knew he wouldn't be pleased if she told him the truth now.

He gaped at her. "Is it a secret?"

"Nooo, not exactly. In fact, they're actually quite well known."

"Well-known secret agents?" he asked skeptically. "You mean like James Bond? The only people who don't seem to know who he is are the poor fools who try to help him."

"No, it's not like that." Alexis closed her mouth suddenly and gave him a pleading look. She felt boxed in, unsure what to say.

"I see," Jace answered, though it was clear that he didn't. "You don't want to talk about your family."

"No." She gave a small shrug. "I don't see how it could be important to my short-term job here."

Jace looked at her for a moment. His eyes went dark and his voice was low. "Did you ever think that maybe my interest isn't because of your job?"

Her lips formed a silent "O." The awareness of him that she had been trying to hold off tingled through her. Suddenly, she felt the heat his big body generated, the muscled strength of his arm. She smelled his scent which seemed somehow to be both intimate and woodsy.

His mouth tilted in a way that made her whole world tilt. Following it with her gaze, her head angled to one side and her eyes lifted to meet his. This was a mistake, she thought vaguely. She was now at a perfect angle to kiss him.

Jace seemed to have that same thought. He leaned forward and she could feel the softness of his breath against her lips.

"Hey, Jace," Rocky called out. His feet thudded across the floor.

Jace and Alexis sprang apart. She gasped for air. What had come over her? Had she been about to kiss him? She saw a flicker of confusion in his eyes that matched hers. He surged to his feet as Rocky barreled into the room.

"Jace, I think you'd better come take a look at these steaks. Gil's poked them with a fork about twelve times and they're not bleeding anymore so I think they must be done."

"I'm coming." Then he paused and said, "I...I think we'd better try some ice on that eye." Swinging around, he strode from the room.

Wide-eyed, Alexis watched him go. Her heart sank as she thought of how foolish she must have sounded. She murmured, "Bring me a big bucket of that ice so I can stick my whole head in it."

When both men were gone, Alexis slumped against the sofa back and groaned. Where was her good judgment? Had she left it behind in Inbourg? She *couldn't* be attracted to Jace. She was only here for a short time. He was her boss, and they were from such different worlds, there couldn't possibly be any future in it.

She had to get a grip here, she thought. She had to keep her goals in mind. Experience was what she'd come here for—*teaching* experience, and that was the only kind that interested her. Well, maybe that wasn't strictly true, she admitted with her usual honesty, but it was the only type she was going to pursue.

She touched her fingers gingerly to her eye. Oh, why couldn't Jace have been an ugly, rough old cowboy with bad teeth from chewing tobacco, and a face burned leathery from the sun? Why did he have to be virile and strong and good-looking? And worst of all, smart?

Uncomfortably, she recalled his questions about her family. She fervently hoped he didn't ask again. She simply couldn't lie and she couldn't tell the truth, either. At least, not yet.

"Here," Jace said, shoving a plastic bag loaded with ice at Rocky. "Take this to Alexis."

Rocky looked at Jace as if he was offering the crown jewels, then at the ice, then at his brother. "You bet, Jace." He grabbed the bag with alacrity.

"Hey," Gil protested. "I could have done that. Why don't you let me instead of him?"

Jace's temper, which had been simmering below the surface since he'd realized how close he'd come to kissing Alexis, hit the top of the thermometer and boiled over. "Now listen to me you two blockheads," he snarled. "I've had it with you. You have been acting like a couple of fools ever since she came to Sleepy River. You've harassed her and embarrassed her, and now you've caused her to have a black eye."

"We didn't do that," Gil protested. "It was…"

"Never mind!" Jace thundered even as one part of his brain reminded him how many ways a man could make himself look like an idiot in the space of ten minutes. "What you're going to do now is give her some space and you're going to stop fighting over her."

"Or?" Rocky asked, even though his Adam's apple was bobbing so alarmingly Jace feared for an instant that he might choke.

"Or you can find work somewhere other than the Running M."

Both boys' mouths dropped open and horror bloomed in their eyes. "You mean you'll fire us?" Gil asked.

"In a heartbeat." Jace tried for his sternest look. It wasn't hard since he was feeling as mean as a rattlesnake, anyway.

Hell, it wasn't their fault they were falling all over her, making fools of themselves. He was doing the same thing.

He wondered how long it took for a man to receive absolute confirmation that he was losing his mind.

Chapter Seven

It took Alexis almost four hours to get to sleep after her evening with Jace and the Patchett brothers, though it wasn't because of anything Gil and Rocky had done. To her amazement, the boys had settled down and treated her with the utmost courtesy. Best of all, they'd stopped fighting over her. She intercepted an occasional fierce look passing between them, and she was almost certain she had seen Rocky try to stab his brother's hand with a fork after he had passed the butter to her, but she wasn't sure.

Jace had been the soul of courtesy, as well, Alexis admitted. She was sitting on her bed, having found a comfortable place to settle between the lumps and bumps of her old mattress. She had her legs crossed and her elbows resting on her knees in as unladylike a pose as she ever assumed. She was staring grumpily into the darkness outside her window.

Jace had been the perfect host, serving the slightly overcooked, but still delicious steak with smooth efficiency. He had been the ultimate gentleman. It wasn't his fault she had misinterpreted the occasional steely looks he had given her and blushed to the roots of her hair.

She had almost kissed him. Alexis flopped back against her pillow and groaned out loud. She couldn't imagine what had been going through her mind. Nothing, obviously, except a need to be closer to him, to taste his mouth and see if it was as exciting as she suspected. And what was she doing even thinking about his mouth?

She couldn't do something as disastrous as become involved with him by so much as a little kiss. Or a big one, either.

And it wasn't only because he was the chairman of the school board. It was also that she was going to be gone in a few months. She would never be back. Once her father found out that she had been teaching school rather than pampering herself at a spa, it was doubtful that she would ever return to the United States—or even be allowed off the grounds of the palace. There was a family story that Hedrick the Henchman had locked up a wandering wife. There was a room in the dungeon that looked far too comfortable for a prisoner or jailer. Prince Michael might decide it was the perfect place for his rebellious daughter. He would hold her prisoner in Inbourg until he found her a suitable husband.

"Ugh!" Alexis said out loud, and rolled over onto her stomach. She didn't want a husband from the choice of men her father had picked out. They were either minor royalty from neighboring countries or businessmen more interested in the possible prestige that marriage to a princess of Inbourg would bring. They weren't interested in her personally. They didn't even *know* her.

But Prince Michael had put out the casting call for a husband for his youngest daughter and the candidates had begun to line up.

He was absolutely determined that she wouldn't follow in her wayward sisters' footsteps. Alexis wasn't sure why her father thought she would suddenly turn docile when she had always been the one with her own ideas and plans. No doubt, desperation had prompted his lineup of candidates for her hand.

She couldn't imagine Jace standing in that lineup. If he loved her, he would move right to the head of it and toss out all others.

Alexis indulged in a momentary daydream that resembled the old fairy tale about the princess on the glass hill. The man who climbed the slippery slope successfully would win the hand of the princess. She imagined Jace on Hondo, charging up the hill to sweep her away. He would do that, too, if he loved her.

If he loved her. *Loved her?*

She was hallucinating. The stressful beginning of school, a black eye and her attraction to Jace were unhinging her mind. There was no other explanation since she had never been the type of woman who wanted to be rescued from anything. She had always preferred to go her own way, do her own thing, which was why she had attended university in Arizona, and, of course, was how she'd ended up teaching in a one-room schoolhouse in the White Mountains.

She liked being independent and self-reliant. As much as she loved her sisters, she didn't want to be like them, depending first on their father, and then on the men they seemed to fall in love with on a regular basis. Both Anya and Deirdre had wanted to be out of the unrelenting glare of the public eye, and to keep Jean Louis out of it, even though she knew that as heir to the throne, that would never happen. That's why Anya had looked for a wealthy man to help shield her.

Alexis was different. She didn't want anyone to rescue her, not even Jace.

Sitting in the dark, with her chin propped in her palms, she reconfirmed that decision. She didn't need rescuing by him. But oh, he was so strong, so masculine and sure of himself. And yet his touch had been so gentle when he'd been tending to her eye.

Alexis grabbed her pillow and held it against the heat swelling in her chest. She felt dangerously close to tears and it had nothing to do with her sore eye. Never in her life had she agonized over a man this way. For one thing, she didn't know all that many. She hadn't dated very much. Alarmed by her sisters' exploits, her father's careful watch on Alexis had guaranteed that few boys or young men made the attempt to get to know her.

Therefore, nothing had prepared her for Jace.

She couldn't pursue this attraction, anyway, because once he found out the truth about her, he would feel that she had lied. Lying had been the furthest thing from her mind. She had only wanted to teach, to gain some much-needed experience to take back home with her, and do it in a place where she wasn't known, and in a way where her family name and history wouldn't influence people around her. She had wanted to be accepted for herself.

But if it came up, how could she explain that to Jace?

Alexis's troubled sleep was interrupted by the ringing of her cell phone. She fumbled for it on her small nightstand and squinted at the buttons through her swollen lid.

Gingerly, she tested the area around her eye with one hand as she mumbled "Hello," into the phone.

"Alexis?" her father's voice boomed in her ear so loudly, she had the urge to snap to attention and salute. She did manage to sit bolt upright in alarm.

"Dad?" she quavered, then was annoyed with herself for her wimpy tone. She cleared her throat and tried again, but it sounded just as bad the second time.

"What's the matter with you?" he demanded. "Are they working you too hard there?"

Still foggy with sleep, she stumbled over words. "No, Dad, the children are very well-behaved, and..." Finally, a few brain molecules came alive and she gulped back the rest of what she'd been about to say.

"Children? Alexis, what are you talking about?"

"Nothing," she said hastily. "Nothing, Dad. I was...dreaming. You woke me."

"Well, that's good," he responded in his imperious way. "You're supposed to be getting rested up and healthy, but you sound like you're sick. You aren't sick, are you?"

"No, Dad, I'm not." She pulled the covers up to her chin, wishing that she was dressed, or had at least brushed her hair. Somehow it was easier to face her father, even on the phone, if she was dressed. She knew the best way to head him off the subject of her health was to ask about the family. "How is everyone? How does Jean Louis like school?" It was his first year, and she regretted having to miss hearing about his daily experiences.

"Everyone's fine. Jean Louis is the smartest boy they've ever had at that school," Prince Michael responded proudly. In a burst of democratic fervor after the approval of the revised constitution, he had insisted that Anya enroll her son at the local school. For the first time, a member of the royal family was attending classes with the children who lived near the palace. Although she had approved his action, Alexis had been secretly dismayed because the school officials seemed to be satisfied with low academic standards. It was one of the things she hoped to change.

"He likes it fine there. Loves school and gets along with the other children even though he threatened to put one of them in the dungeon for taking a toy he wanted to play with."

Alexis laughed. How she missed the little stinker.

"Deirdre's got a new boyfriend," Prince Michael went on with annoyance. "Some horse breeder."

Probably owns a string of successful stables, Alexis

thought to herself. Her sister always chose successful men and Prince Michael insisted on viewing them as upstart nobodies simply because they weren't his choice. She tried to get more information about the man, but he cut her off.

"I didn't call to report on the family."

Uh-oh, here it comes. She sat up straight and braced herself.

"I want to know how long you're going to be at that place," he went on.

"I thought we agreed you would let me have some time to myself," she hedged.

"I am," he thundered. "I simply want to know when you're going to come home."

She took a deep breath. "Three months."

"Three months?" His voice rose. "What on earth are you going to do in that place for three months?"

Her hands twisted in the sheets, but she forged on. "That's beside the point. You said I could have this time for myself."

"But three months? You've already been gone for three weeks."

"Dad, I spent a full year doing exactly what you wanted me to do. I stayed and watched out for Jean Louis so you and Anya and Deirdre could concentrate on the constitution and all the public relations involved in selling it to the country."

"Well, yes, but..."

"And when the constitution was passed, Anya took Jean Louis and went cruising on Stavros Andarko's yacht. Deirdre went to Ireland where she's apparently met this horse breeder. I stayed home because that's what you wanted me to do. Well, now I'm doing what I want and I'll be home soon enough."

There was a lengthy silence from Prince Michael. Finally, he spoke, calmer now. "All right," he finally answered. "You're going to get what you want, but..."

"What?" she asked hesitantly.

"You've never spent five minutes pampering yourself in your life, and now...three months?"

Alexis could picture him shaking his head in wonder. "I'll be home before you know it, Dad."

"Just be sure you do, and tell Esther I expect her to look out for you. I don't want to find out in one of those damned rag newspapers that you've gotten yourself tangled up with some beefcake boyfriend." With a hasty goodbye, he hung up, while Alexis choked in surprise.

"A beefcake boyfriend?" she sputtered. "I can't even have a beef-*raising* one." Not that Jace had indicated he wanted to be in that capacity.

She swung her feet to the floor and stood, heading for the mirror in the bathroom that would tell her how bad her eye was.

When she had moved into the teacherage, she had been pleasantly surprised to discover that it had a remarkably modern and efficient bathroom. Now that oh-so-efficient mirror showed her bruised eye in all its purple splendor. She grimaced. "Billy Saunders is going to tell all the other kids I've been in a fight, and he'll entertain the whole school with the imaginary details." And darn it, she would be as enthralled as the children with his tale.

Even the truth would sound strange, that she had bumped into Jace's elbow. She wouldn't tell them that, she decided suddenly. Maybe she wouldn't tell them anything at all. Maybe she would assign them to write an essay entitled, "How Miss Chastain Got Her Black Eye." The younger students could draw a picture of it. Even the efforts of a kindergartner wouldn't look much worse than this.

Another piece of truth she wouldn't share with them was how she was falling for the school board chairman. She certainly wouldn't tell them that her heart seemed to leap for joy whenever she saw him, that she found him wildly attractive, that she'd desperately wanted to kiss him last night.

How on earth had things become so complicated, anyway?

"That's a complicated knot you've gotten yourself tangled up in, Jace."

Jace glanced around to see Luke Braden observing him. His fellow rancher had ridden over from his place across the ridge and now sat easily atop his big roan mare as he watched Jace untangle a snarl of twine. It had become caught in the blades of the mower he was using to knock down the weeds between the trees in the orchard. It wasn't a job he relished, nor was it one that particularly needed to be done. He was only doing it because he felt a peculiar need to punish himself.

He had almost kissed Alexis, kissed her with Gil and Rocky three rooms away, kissed her while she'd been suffering from a black eye that he'd given her.

Because he wanted to snap at himself, he spoke to his old friend with unnecessary harshness.

"If you came by to tell me what I already know, you might as well leave."

"And miss the show?" Luke asked easily, sliding from the saddle. "Wouldn't dream of it." Grinning, he strode up, shucked a many-bladed knife from his pocket, and said, "Here."

Jace took it without a word of thanks, and flipped out one of the sharp blades which sliced smoothly through the twine.

"How'd that get caught in the blades, anyway?" Luke asked.

"I ran over it."

"Don't you usually watch where you're going?"

Jace gave him a poisonous look. "Who would have thought to look for baling twine clear out here?"

"I don't know, but I expect if you'd asked either of your hired doofuses if they'd recently dropped some, they would have said, 'Oh, yeah. It jumped out of the truck and went to take a nap under the apple tree.'"

Unexpectedly, Jace grinned. Luke had a talent for mimicry and had sounded exactly like the Patchetts. "No doubt."

"I don't know why you keep those two on."

"Because their dad is an old friend and I'm obliged to him for hauling my butt out of debt a few years ago."

Luke swiped a long blade of grass from the ground and began chewing on it.

"So you have to pay for it by putting up with Gil and Rocky?"

"They're good hands," Jace defended.

"As long as you never take your eyes off of them."

Jace couldn't deny that, so he said nothing while he finished with the twine, bundled it out of the way, and then prepared to restart the mower.

"You take things too personally and too seriously."

Jace frowned. "I told you, I'm obliged to their dad for helping me out."

Luke only shook his head and Jace knew exactly what he was thinking. They'd had this discussion off and on most of their lives.

"And you have to take on Gil and Rocky because it somehow proves to the world that you're not like your old man, not hard and cold, willing to take on a couple of barely adequate men and put up with their shenanigans...."

Jace cut him off with a hard look. "Why did you say you stopped by?"

"I didn't." Luke glanced around, his dark eyes curious. "Billy tells me the new schoolteacher is quite a looker."

Jace grunted, ignoring the surge of jealousy that stabbed him. "You're taking the word of a ten-year-old?"

"Hey, Billy might be a handful, but he's got good eyes." Luke grew serious. "Nah, the truth is, my nephew, Brad, might be coming to stay with me for a while."

Jace straightened. "Raina's little boy?"

"Yeah. She's decided to go to medical school and she figures she can't do that and raise a kid."

The two men exchanged a long look. Jace knew his old friend was sharing his thoughts, that Luke's brilliant but self-centered sister should never have had a child.

She should never have run off from Sleepy River, married the first guy she met, had Brad the next year, and then flitted away from her husband, wagging the baby along with her. For his part, Jace never should have been infatuated with her to the point where he thought he'd suffered a broken heart when she'd left. After telling himself no woman would matter to him as much as the Running M, his heart had healed so quickly, he'd known it had never been broken, but his experience with Raina had left him wary.

"So, tell me what Miss Chastain is like," Luke commanded, chewing thoughtfully on the blade of grass.

Now there's a question, Jace thought, leaning against the mower handle.

"She's qualified to teach here. Martha said so," he answered with a shrug.

"And?"

"She seems to be doing an okay job. The kids like her."

"I already know that much from Billy," Luke answered. "I mean what kind of woman is she?"

The prickle of jealousy became a sharp jab in the gut. "Why? Are you thinking of asking her out?"

Luke rocked back on his heels and gave Jace an interested look. "Why? Is she worth asking out?"

Jace didn't answer because he had no answer. Instead, he leaned over to grab the starter handle and give the rope a tug. "Sure," he said. "I guess." Then he cut off further conversation by jerking on the rope and starting the motor to life with a roar.

When he turned the mower to finish the job, he saw that Luke had remounted his horse, though he seemed to be having some difficulty since he was laughing so hard. With a wave, he rode off toward the schoolhouse.

Angrily, Jace stalked along behind the handle, pushing the mower back and forth at warp speed, imagining Luke riding up to the door of the teacherage, dismounting, meeting Alexis, charming her, commiserating with her over her black eye.

Her black eye!

Jace stopped so fast he left skid marks in the grass. He stood perfectly still while he stared straight ahead and the mower's motor put-putted noisily.

He hadn't even asked about her black eye that day. He could have called her, or ridden Hondo through the woods to call on her, or even driven the truck over. In fact, he *should* have done that. He was the one who had caused her injury and the one who had doctored it. The least he could do was go find out if it was healing up.

Jace did something he never would have allowed Gil or Rocky to do—abandoned his equipment where it stood and raced for the house.

Chapter Eight

Alexis laughed up at the charming cowboy who had dropped by to meet her and stayed to drink lemonade with her on her front porch.

"Now, old Jace, you want to watch out for him," Luke said, his eyes twinkling.

Alexis sat back, tucked her tongue into her cheek, and wrapped her hands around her glass of lemonade. It was a hot day so she had put on shorts and a tank top to sit outside in the hope of catching a breeze. She had been studying up on social studies for the two fifth-graders—her knowledge of European history was better than her knowledge of American history—when Luke Braden had arrived. She'd felt self-conscious because her hair was in an untidy topknot. Luke didn't seem to care, though. He'd given her a long, interested look, then begun talking about Jace.

She smiled now at Luke's assessment of him. "Why is that?"

"Well, he's just a tad on the possessive side, and he's way too responsible. He thinks he has to keep an eye on everything that's going on around this community. Anything that's even remotely connected to his ranch, well, he feels responsible for it, then he starts getting possessive, wanting to keep people close to him so he can make sure they're all right."

"Like Gil and Rocky?" Alexis asked in a mild tone. She had heard about Jace's overdeveloped sense of responsibility from Jace himself, but it was interesting to hear Luke's views, as well.

"Among others." Luke grinned and drained his glass. He waved off her offer of more and set the glass on the railing by his hip.

Alexis liked him. He was a tall, rangy cowboy, not as powerful in the arms and shoulders as Jace, but was whipcord lean instead. Beneath the brim of his recklessly tilted black cowboy hat, she could see that his hair was a dark auburn. Like Jace, he had a deep tan and lines raying out from the corners of his eyes. He was more easygoing, though, with a grin that came and went heart-stoppingly fast. He was a charmer, all right, and she could just imagine that somewhere in his past lurked a Mississippi riverboat gambler.

She could tell that he liked Jace, and so she liked Luke right away.

"Tell me about your nephew, Luke. Do you expect him to be arriving soon?"

"Probably this week." Luke launched into the odd

history of his eight-year-old nephew's life, his many changes of homes and schools as his mother took him from one part of the country to another, changing jobs, changing boyfriends, changing her mind.

"Raina is…restless," Luke concluded, and sadness filled his face.

"It can be hard for kids when they have no say over what happens to them," Alexis said sympathetically.

"Or about who raises them," Luke responded. "Like Jace," he added, and Alexis caught a shrewd look in his eyes.

She couldn't resist the bait. "What about Jace?"

She saw a quietly satisfied gleam in Luke's eye as if she'd done something to please him. "His mother left these mountains when he was only ten. She couldn't live with the isolation anymore so she moved to town. She tried to take Jace with her, but Jace's dad wouldn't let her. She only got him on weekends and holidays. It was an unusual arrangement for the time, but the judge was a crony of Tom McTaggart's, so the old man got what he wanted."

But what had Jace wanted? she wondered. Sadly, Alexis formed a mental picture of Jace as a little boy, dark hair falling into brown eyes that watched the world cautiously.

"It was rough on Jace," Luke went on. "Being shuttled back and forth between his parents and raised mostly by his father wasn't easy. He was a demanding perfectionist. He had to be right about everything. I think that's one of the reasons Jace puts up with Gil and Rocky. They can't do much, but he praises them like crazy for anything they *can* do. Then, when they screw up, he feels responsible." Luke shook his head. "Funny guy."

Alexis had more questions about Jace, but Luke tilted his head suddenly and said, "Speak of the devil."

"What? Oh!" She looked across the school yard to see Jace emerge from the head of the path that led to his house. He was riding Hondo, who cantered easily across the ball field and came to a stop at Alexis's porch.

"Luke," he said with a nod. "I didn't know you'd still be here."

Luke chuckled. "Oh, I'll just bet."

The tips of Jace's ears took on a definitely pink hue that delighted Alexis. He ignored his friend and looked at her. "Thought I'd better check on your eye. Is it all right?"

Automatically self-conscious, she lifted her hand to her eye, which Luke had been gentleman enough not to mention. The swelling had gone down and it looked better than it had that morning, but it was still sensitive. "It's better. I've decided to use it as a creative writing exercise—'How Miss Chastain Got Her Black Eye,'" she told them ruefully.

"I want to read Billy's story," Luke said, pushing away from the porch railing. "It's bound to be exciting." He set his glass on the tray beside Alexis and said, "I'll be going now. Expect my nephew in a week or so, Alexis. Thanks for the lemonade. See ya, Jace," he said casually as he walked to his horse.

As he mounted and rode away, Alexis looked expectantly at Jace. "Would you like some lemonade?" she asked, then felt foolish for some reason. She had been perfectly comfortable offering it to Luke, but with Jace, well, it somehow seemed as if she was begging him to stay.

"Thanks," he said easily, dismounting and leaving Hondo to graze on the grass that edged the porch. He climbed the steps, removing his hat and brushing it against his thigh to knock out the dust. He took Luke's place on the porch railing while Alexis went inside for another glass. As she reached into the cabinet, it struck her that he was the most welcome guest she'd had in her little temporary home. She was delighted that he'd come to visit her, and to see about her black eye, even though she realized that he probably only saw her as another of his responsibilities.

When she came out of the house, she saw his long-legged figure perched precariously on the railing and said, "I'm sorry there's only one chair."

She didn't offer it to him because she knew he was too much of a gentleman to accept.

He lifted an eyebrow at her in a look that was both rueful and humored. "I'm the one who should be sorry," he said. "We should have provided some porch furniture for you."

She smiled as she handed him his glass and seated herself. She stretched her legs out, reveling in the freedom and comfort she felt. "It doesn't matter. I'm usually here alone."

He frowned and she swiftly added, "I'm not lonely, though. It's nice being on my own." If he only knew *how* nice.

"This kind of quiet and solitude isn't for everyone," he said, looking around at the pine and aspen that edged the clearing.

"But it's right for you, isn't it, Jace?"

He turned his head and gave her a steady look. "It's where I belong."

"The luckiest people in the world are the ones who learn early on exactly where it is that they belong," she murmured.

"Sounds like you're quoting someone."

"My mother," she admitted with a tremble of longing in her voice. She took a sip of lemonade to steady herself. "She died when I was fifteen."

"I'm sorry," he said. "My mother is alive, but she lives in Tucson, so I don't see her much. She's not too crazy about these mountains."

Although she already knew that, Alexis hoped he would tell her more, but he fell into a reflective silence. "Then this wasn't the place where she belonged."

"How about you?" he asked suddenly. He leaned forward and set his glass down. "Where do you belong?"

Here, she almost said, then realized with a shock that it was true. Or, at least she wanted to belong here. She loved the quiet, the easy pace, the interesting, challenging work that was so much more to her liking than smiling her way through a reception for the ambassador from some country whose politics she abhorred.

Her heart sank with the realization that she would be gone in only a matter of months, back to standing up to her father in the matter of a suitable marriage, to trying to fight the battle of better schools for Inbourg, to the life she had always known, and would always know. She looked down, sadly aware that there were certain duties she could never escape.

Most of the time she didn't resent the life that was ahead of her. She was proud of her family and her heritage, proud to be a member of a family that had ruled at least passably well for three hundred years. But there were times, like now, when she could have given it all up.

It shook her to the core to contemplate the thoughts that were going through her head. There was no indication that Jace felt the same way about her, but she had the inevitable feeling that she was falling in love with him.

Shakily, she set her glass down, rattling the ice cubes, sloshing the liquid over the rim and onto her hand.

For days she had let her mind flirt with the idea of her attraction to Jace, but this was more than attraction she was feeling now—and it was completely inappropriate.

In slow motion, she lifted her hand to lick off the tartly sweet drink.

"Alexis?" Jace said, and she lifted her stricken eyes to see that he was standing in front of her. She hadn't even heard him move. "What's wrong?"

His rugged face was full of concern as he knelt down, his knees widespread, his backside resting on his heels. He looked at her for several long moments as if he was trying to see into her mind, then he reached out and grasped both of her hands.

"What's the matter, Alexis? You look like you've seen a ghost."

Lips pressed together, she shook her head because she couldn't speak without saying something foolish. The feel of his hands, big and callused, wrapped around hers was making her even more confused.

Gently he pulled, scooting her forward from the chair, and into his arms. He sat, drawing her with him until he was sitting with his back against a wooden post.

Surprised and elated, she went willingly, feeling his strength surround her.

"I didn't mean to upset you," he said, his voice a low rumble in the quiet air.

"You didn't...I..." Alexis looked into his warm brown eyes and her heart jolted into a rapid beat. "I was just thinking that I wished I belonged here in Sleepy River."

She saw something flare in his eyes, but it was quickly damped down as if he intended to keep hope in check. "You don't think this is the place for you?"

She shook her head as her eyes filled with tears. "I don't have the freedom to say that."

"What do you mean? It's a free country. You can go wherever you want. Stay wherever you want."

Her lips trembled. "Some of us are more free than others."

"Alexis, I..." His words failed as he reached up and brushed away a tear that trailed down her cheek.

Faced with this endearing uncertainty from such a

strong man, Alexis felt something tremble and break inside her. She was dangerously close to falling in love with him. It was exhilarating and terrifying and she didn't think she could tell him about it, but there it was.

Acting on her feelings, she leaned forward, slipped her arms around his neck and did what she'd been wanting to do. She placed her lips on his and kissed him.

His mouth was firm, as strong as the rest of him, and yet soft and giving as if the generosity of his nature had a physical outlet.

After the first few moments of shock, Jace gathered her to him and took over the kiss. It was frightening and powerful and wonderful to have him holding and kissing her. Alexis's heart pounded against her throat with such excitement she thought it might burst through.

"Alexis," he murmured, trailing kisses across her face, tenderly placing one on her bruised eye. "You've been driving me crazy since the night you tried to burn me out."

"I didn't," she countered on a laughing protest. She drew away to see the teasing light in his eyes. "That dry grass just happened to be in the wrong place at the wrong time."

He grinned, then his smile smoothed into a puzzled look. "I don't know anything about you but I can't stop thinking about you. I ask you questions, but you won't tell me anything about your background and family."

"Because you're a man who doesn't like surprises

and deceptions,'' she responded. Her mouth had gone dry and dread was settling into her stomach.

He went very still. "No, I don't.'' His gaze searched her face, an easy task since it was only inches from his.

Alexis felt that everything was rushing in on her, that she was helpless to stop the next words that would be coming from her mouth. She took a deep breath. "Jace, have you ever heard of a country named Inbourg?''

Jace stared at her, dumbfounded. "A princess? You're a princess?'' It wasn't the first time he'd said it. Or the second.

"Guilty as charged.''

"Royalty? Heir to the throne and all that?''

Alexis answered with a tiny shrug. "Only if, God forbid, something should happen to Anya and her son Jean Louis, and my other sister, Deirdre. I'm only fourth in line.''

He had felt numb at first when she had carefully and succinctly told him what he'd wanted to know about her family and background. Now his curiosity was satisfied, but he felt something else growing inside, something that felt unpleasantly like betrayal.

What had he been thinking, he mocked himself, that she would stay on after her job was finished? Stay with him? What a joke.

Before he could make an even bigger fool of himself, he set her away from him, turning from the sudden dismay in her eyes.

"Why didn't you tell me all this when you first

came?" He got to his feet, then because she looked so small and vulnerable sitting on the porch floor, and he felt guilty for putting that distress on her face, he reached down and pulled her to her feet, as well, then let go of her and stood back. Because he couldn't meet her eyes, he turned and paced away from her, down the length of the shabby porch. He crossed his arms over his chest and waited.

"I didn't know you," she stammered, holding out her hands, palms up. "And our first meeting wasn't all that...comfortable."

She stepped away from him to the other end of the porch, and it seemed as if she'd leaped to the other side of a chasm. He had pulled himself away from her warmth and he felt chilled without it, but she hadn't been honest with him. It was a huge stumbling block to him. She was right, he didn't like surprises and deceptions. It reeked of what he'd once heard from his parents so long ago, *"Don't tell your father, but..."* or *"Your mother doesn't need to know about this, son...."*

He thought he'd left all that, and all his resentments behind him, but somehow it hurt more coming from Alexis.

He knew she was alarmed by the severe look on his face, but he couldn't seem to change it. Hondo had kicked him in the stomach once when he'd been a colt and Jace felt that same breath-stealing sickness now.

She stumbled on with her explanation. "There are other issues, too, Jace. There are other people I don't want to know I'm here."

"Who?" he asked, feeling a spurt of jealousy. "Jet-setting boyfriends?"

"Tabloids," she shot back, throwing her hands wide. "They would love to get a story about me teaching in a one-room schoolhouse in the mountains."

Somehow that struck him as the greatest betrayal of all. "I'd think you'd like that kind of publicity. Magnanimous princess teaching the isolated children of backwards mountain folk."

Hurt flared in her eyes, followed by fury. She drew herself up and gave him the look he thought was probably described as being the royal freeze. "If you think that," she said in a tone her ancestors must have once used to send men to the gallows, "then you know less than nothing about me."

"You're damned right about that." Seething, confused, and feeling like a fool, he snatched up his hat and turned toward Hondo. His boot heels pummeled the wooden stairs as he descended them. He grabbed Hondo's reins so suddenly the gelding started and whinnied, but Jace vaulted onto his back. "Thanks for the lemonade," he said. "And the buggy ride." Pulling his horse's head around, he nudged him with his heels and galloped for home.

"Oaf!" Alexis shouted after him, richly furious. "Idiot!"

She went into the house and slammed the door. "Ooooh," she ranted, taking several quick turns around the room. She'd known he wouldn't like what she had to tell him. He didn't like dishonesty in any form. However, she hadn't expected him to act as if she had betrayed him. She had always thought he was a fair man—look at what he put up with from Gil and Rocky. She had at least thought he would listen to her explanation.

Her fury drained away and disappointment filled her. She sat down heavily on the old sofa and propped her chin in her hands. She felt betrayed, too, because she had misread him. It was obvious that she understood him far less than she thought she did, not that her experience with the opposite sex had been vast enough to give her much insight.

In spite of what the rest of the world thought, she and her sisters weren't the jet-setters they were often portrayed to be. Their father had sheltered them, especially after the death of their mother, Princess Charlotte. In fact, if he'd given them more freedom, Anya might not have married the first exciting man she met, Deirdre might be less of a flirt, and Alexis perhaps wouldn't have grown up so determined to go her own way and be her own person.

Even during her college years, her activities had been restricted by what people would think. Her presence at the university in Phoenix had been kept quiet, her social life limited.

Still, she thought as she pushed herself to her feet and returned to the porch to retrieve the lemonade tray, she'd thought she had enough understanding of human nature to know how Jace would react to what she had told him.

Obviously, she'd been wrong.

It seemed as if this entire adventure had been

blighted from the beginning. First she'd had to be less than honest with her father about her real reason for going to Arizona. She needed to confront him, tell him she had no intention of marrying any of his candidates. She should tell him, in the most loving possible way, of course, to stick to running Inbourg and let her run her life.

She was reluctant to do that, though, because he would be hurt. He saw his interference in his children's lives as his duty, the act of a loving parent.

Alexis reached up and rubbed her forehead with her fingertips, then carefully tested the tender area around her eye. Thank goodness the bruise would be healed by the time she reached home or she would never hear the end of the questions from him.

She would certainly have a talk with him about his need to micromanage her, but right now, she had things to do. Straightening her shoulders and holding her head up, Alexis gave a regal nod. She had many things to do.

The first week of school had been hard—okay, it had been nearly impossible—but she was determined to improve. Let Jace be angry with her all he wanted. Let him think she had betrayed him somehow. He wasn't going to be able to say she hadn't done her job.

Grabbing the key to the schoolhouse, she marched next door and began to furiously make plans and preparations.

"Miss Chastain, are you okay?" Becky Kramer stared up at her teacher, concern in her small, freckled face. "How come you don't have on a pretty dress like you wore last week?" Dismayed, she eyed Alexis's jeans and T-shirt.

Oh, great, Alexis thought ruefully as she looked into those big, blue eyes. She was even managing to disappoint the youngest members of the community, though maybe not as much as she had disappointed Jace. She stiffened her resolve, refusing to think about him. He'd invaded her thoughts and dreams enough over the weekend. It was now Monday, the students were all ready to begin lessons, and she was ready to teach.

She bent down to give the small girl a hug. "We're going to have a lesson on statistics today," she said. "And in order to do that, we need to play baseball. And I can't play in a dress." Actually, she couldn't play at all, but the kids would be learning that soon enough. She'd spent all day Sunday with a book of baseball tactics and statistics, so she was sure she could do this.

Billy Saunders frowned. "You mean we're going to have a math lesson during the game?" He slumped down in his chair muttering, "That'll be fun."

"Give it a chance, Billy," she answered. In spite of her annoyance with Jace, she had taken his advice and told Billy if it was all right with Martha Single-ton, he could begin gathering information about building and stocking a snake enclosure. Although she was still nervous about having the creatures about, the project was sure to get Billy's cooperation. The very mention of it had improved his behavior by focusing his energy.

Anticipation was high in the classroom that day because it was the first organized game she had allowed. Though they were limited to an abbreviated team, the kids loved to play. They patiently listened to her lesson on statistics and how they were used to determine a player's standing. When she got out the equipment an hour before dismissal time, they were ecstatic. There was nearly a stampede as they headed outside to play.

It wasn't long before everyone, even the youngest children realized that, in spite of her talk about the game, Miss Chastain didn't know how to play.

"No, no, you've got to hold the glove like this if you're going to be a catcher," one of them groused, trying to show her how to angle the glove to catch the ball. She tried the technique she was shown, but still missed the next few pitches and had to waddle after them, wearing all the catcher's equipment.

Who thought this game up, anyway? she wailed inwardly as she tried to scoop up the ball before the runner made it to base. She was so slow, even with all the kids yelling at her, that he made it all the way to home before she figured out where to throw the ball.

She learned quickly that the competitiveness of nine- and ten-year-old boys could be a scary thing. They were all annoyed with her since she was causing them to lose. Billy was the most disgusted because he was pitching.

"Hey, I'm doing my best," she called back cheerfully, though she was sweating and gasping for air. She crouched behind home plate once again thinking that the only good thing to come from this game might be added toning to her thighs.

The next pitch went wild and she scrambled after it.

"Aw come on, Miss Chastain," one of the other boys complained. "You have to hustle."

"You try it," she muttered. "Wearing all this equipment, catching and being umpire is tough...."

"Especially if you don't know what you're doing," a deep voice responded.

She was brought up short by the sight of Jace standing at the edge of the backstop. She had been so involved in the game, she hadn't even noticed that he had arrived.

She blinked at him through the face guard, feeling foolish. It was one thing to look silly in front of a bunch of kids. She certainly didn't want to look that way in front of him, of all people.

In spite of the sweat rolling into her eyes through a powdering of dust, she gave him a cold look and said, "When I want your opinion, I'll give it to you."

He grinned at her unexpectedly snippy tone. "Why don't you let me show you what to do?"

"No thanks, I'm doing fine without you."

"Hey, Jace," Billy said as he and the other kids abandoned their various posts and came running up. "Do you want to play? You can show her what to do."

Jace looked at her and Alexis could feel her face flushing, and not from exertion. "If it's okay with Miss Chastain," he said, his dark eyes mocking.

"No thank you," she repeated automatically.

"This is strictly a school activity, not a community free-for-all." She barely knew what she was saying, but she was furious at him for showing up now when she wasn't at her most competent.

"Ah, come on, Miss Chastain," the older boys wailed and the other kids chimed in.

"You really need his help," Becky Kramer said solemnly. "You don't know how to do this."

"Out of the mouths of babes," Jace whispered.

Alexis gave him a sour look. "All right," she snapped. "You can play."

Shouting with happiness, the kids all ran back to their positions.

Alexis began unstrapping the buckles that held the various pieces of equipment in place. She fumbled with them so much, that Jace crouched down before her to help.

"Why are you here?" she asked furiously, her green eyes snapping. "You rode off the other day as if you were being chased by the hounds of hell...." Alarmed, she glanced around. No one was within earshot. "Why are you here?"

In spite of her reluctance to have him there, she was aware of his big, strong hands brushing her legs as he expertly unfastened the buckles. She forced herself not to feel pleasure at his touch.

Jace looked up and smiled a smile tinged with self-deprecation. "I'm the school board chairman, remember? I'm supposed to keep an eye on what's going on."

"I don't need you spying on me. I'm doing fine."

"Except at baseball."

She didn't answer, only looked away toward the trees that edged the field.

"Besides," he went on. "I owe you an apology."

"Baseball baseball."

She didn't answer but obviously was forced into
that that old self and find.

Besides," he went on, "I saw you last night.

Chapter Nine

Alexis stared at him. "An apology?" she asked warily. She had spent two nights fretting about what he had said and she wasn't quite sure she was ready to listen to an apology. Besides, to have him stride up as if everything was perfectly all right and act as if he intended to rescue her from her inept baseball catching was galling. She frowned and he raised his eyebrows at her.

"We both know I overreacted the other night," he said.

"Well, *I* certainly know it," she snapped. Hot, dusty and resentful, she wasn't prepared to forgive him too easily. "Why did you react like that?"

He touched the back of his hand to his mouth then tilted his head with a self-deprecating look that was strictly masculine. Those midnight-dark eyes of his held a glint of humor. "I felt like a fool," he said honestly. "And I'm not good at that."

His candidness had her staring at him. He shrugged and she found her annoyance fading. To keep herself from forgiving him too easily, she crossed her arms and tilted her chin at him. "I've found that the more you do something, the better you become at it."

He winced. "You're speaking as a teacher?"

She shook her head. "As one who's made a fool of herself in public places more than once."

He winced. "And had people there to photograph it, right?"

"More times than you can imagine." Was it possible that he was beginning to understand?

Maybe so. He gave her an empathetic look. "How about it? Am I forgiven?"

Before she could answer, Billy shouted, "Hey, Jace, are you gonna talk all day or can we play some baseball?"

Jace waved and shouted, "In a minute. I'm waiting for Miss Chastain to tell me something."

"Well, heck, what's she telling you?" Billy threw his hands in the air and shared a look with his friends who gave disgusted smirks as only adolescent boys can do. "The times tables up to twelve? Backwards? In...in Swahili?"

Jace laughed and glanced back at Alexis. "See? We can't play ball until you forgive me and these other players are getting kind of restless."

"Blackmailer," she said, and then smiled. She took off the face guard and handed it to him. "I accept your apology, but you have to be the catcher."

He grinned and winked at her, then began strapping on the catcher's gear as the kids cheered and whooped. They settled into the game with Jace catching, coaching and umpiring all at the same time, keeping up a running commentary to Alexis on what she needed to look for in order to umpire future games. Alexis called out statistics to the players, praised their performance and generally had the best time of her life.

When the game was over and the children were ready to leave, they chattered happily that school had actually been fun that day. Jace and Alexis shared a laugh at the surprise in their voices.

When everyone had been picked up, Alexis began straightening up the classroom and Jace lingered to help her. It made her smile to see the big, tough cowboy standing by Ginny Garcia's desk with a ponytail scrunchy in his hand. He caught the look on her face, dropped the scrunchy on the desk, and turned to her.

"So, does this mean we're having a truce?"

She folded her hands at her waist and tilted her head. "It looks that way."

"Have you ever negotiated a truce before?" he asked with a teasing smile. "Does your country ever go to war and then send peace envoys out to sign treaties?"

"We fought the Nazis," Alexis said proudly. "We lost, but we fought. We don't have many wars in our background, though. During the Napoleonic Wars some troops from Inbourg went out with the little Corsican to fight the British. Twenty-seven men left and thirty-one came back. They made a few friends along the way.''

"Didn't like fighting for Napoleon, hmm?"

"Oh, they didn't mind that. It was the food they couldn't stand.'' Her green eyes laughed up at him. "We Inbourgians have certain standards that we won't compromise.''

He chuckled. "So you haven't had much experience with war and truces, and all that?''

"Not much,'' she admitted, watching cautiously as he walked slowly toward her. Excitement began to hum inside her when she saw the sleepy gleam in his eyes.

"You also haven't had much experience as a teacher, this being your first real job and all.''

"That's right.'' She tipped her head. "Jace, what exactly is your point?'' She had a feeling she knew what it was and the intent look in his eyes confirmed it.

"I'm only thinking that you seem to need a little educating yourself.''

"In what way?''

"Did you ever kiss a cowboy?''

"Only you,'' she gasped on a spurt of laughter.

"I bet you've never kissed one in your classroom.''

"Certainly not!''

"You're sure?''

"No,'' she said firmly. "And I don't intend to start now.'' She put her hands on her hips. "Are you saying there's something wrong with the way I kiss?''

"Nah.'' His mouth was tilting into a devilish grin.

"Not a thing wrong with it. You seem to know what you're doing...for a beginner."

"A beginner?" Alexis echoed in mock outrage. "I'll have you know that my very first kiss was with Ronald Crookshanks who kissed me in the formal gardens of our palace and it was a hot one, too."

"Oh yeah?" He stopped in front of her, crossed his arms over his chest and rocked on his heels. He tilted that big, square chin of his down and gave her a severe look. "How hot?"

"Hot enough to glue our lips together." Alexis's green eyes sparkled as she laughed up at him. "He's the nephew of Bevins, the palace manager. We were five years old and we'd been eating cinnamon candies." She sighed. "It was a kiss never to be forgotten."

Jace reached out, grasped her by the arms and pulled her to him. "I'll show you a kiss never to be forgotten."

He touched his lips to hers, and laughing softly, she wound her arms around his neck, stretched onto her tiptoes and kissed him back. It started out fun, sweet and gentle, then heated up rapidly. His mouth was so warm and welcoming, she wanted to sink into him, to revel in him. She heard herself moan and wondered vaguely if she should feel embarrassed, but she heard Jace catch his breath and she knew his blood was heating, as well.

Finally, he pulled away and rested his forehead against hers. "You go to my head," he said as if he couldn't quite believe it. "You have since the first minute I saw you standing in my house, covered in soot.''

Alexis groaned. "Please don't remind me. I haven't set fire to anything in weeks now and I'm going to replace that quilt, I swear.''

"I'm not worried," he said.

"But I owe you..."

"Nothing," he said and kissed her again. "I was pretty mad about it at first, but other things have claimed my attention.'' Gently, he touched her black eye. "How are the essays coming along?''

"They're due tomorrow. Older kids have to write two paragraphs. Younger ones are to draw a picture. I think some of them will be pretty graphic.''

He nodded as if he was only half listening, then paused as if choosing his words carefully. "The other day, when you told me who you really are, I acted like a jerk because it matters to me that you level with me.'' His gaze met hers. "I was surprised how much it mattered.''

Touched, overcome with her feelings for him, Alexis lifted her hand to rest it on his cheek. Beneath her palm, she felt the muscles jump. He turned his face and placed a kiss in her hand, then as if shying away from how much of himself he was revealing, he gave her a quirky lift of his brows and asked, "Are you hungry?''

She smiled. "Do you want a snack?''

"Nah. I owe you dinner.''

"It's three-thirty in the afternoon.''

"We'll go into town. By the time we get there, it'll be dinnertime.''

Happiness filled her eyes. "Is this a date?"

Jace shook his head as if he couldn't quite believe it himself. "Yeah, I guess it is. Though how I'm going to explain this to Gil and Rocky is something I don't know. They're both in love with you, you know."

I wish you were, Alexis thought, then blinked in surprise at herself. She'd never put that thought into words before and she wished she had time to explore it, but Jace went on.

"Alexis, you knew that," he prompted, reacting to the look of surprise on her face.

"It's a crush," she said. "Because I'm the only single woman around."

"Except for Hattie Fritz, but she's nearly eighty and she likes bees more than humans." He paused, waiting. "So how about it? Wanna have dinner with a crabby old cowboy who doesn't come down out of the mountains very often?"

There were all kinds of reasons she shouldn't do this, she told herself. She was a teacher and he was in charge of the school board. She was only going to be in Sleepy River temporarily and he would never leave it. In spite of the independence she wanted to establish for herself, her family responsibilities would always bind her, whereas Jace had no family, but was bound by huge responsibilities right here at his ranch.

All kinds of reasons to say no, and only one to say yes—her heart was telling her to because she was falling in love with him. She smiled. "Yes. Even though it's a school night and I've got lessons to prepare. I'd love to."

* * *

Although they were sure no one had seen them leave Sleepy River together, their date didn't remain a secret for as long as twelve hours. Becky Kramer came to school the next morning, stared at Alexis curiously, then giggled, showing the place where she'd recently lost a tooth. "Are you gonna marry Jace?"

Alexis, who had just opened the front door to let the short line of children inside blinked down at the little girl. Other kids were giggling now, the boys poking and elbowing each other as they waited for her answer.

"Are you, huh, Miss Chastain?" one of the boys asked.

"If you did, I bet he'd let you ride his horse," the school's one and only second-grader said brightly. She loved horses and drew spindly pictures of them along the margins of all her papers.

Good grief, she thought, these kids could be as curious as the dreaded tabloid reporters. She opened her mouth to respond, but was unexpectedly rescued by Billy, who sauntered forward and said, "They've only had one date. A guy's not supposed to ask until they've been going out awhile." His worldly wise air seemed to convince the others who giggled a little more and trooped inside. Billy gave her a conspiratorial nod and followed.

Alexis still hadn't spoken a word, but she didn't need to since Billy had seemingly settled the matter. After their baseball game, she had told him he could definitely build a snake house outside the school and maintain it. He'd been elated and now she was his favorite teacher ever. She had to remember to thank Jace for that advice when he came over later.

Happily, she went about her work, teaching and directing the children, but always in the back of her mind were memories of their evening together. It had been wonderful to be with him, to talk and laugh without the constraints that had pulled at them since they had first met. Best of all, in the small restaurant off the edge of the highway, she hadn't had to worry about a photographer popping out of a potted plant and snapping pictures of her and her date as they had dipped tortilla chips into salsa and munched as they talked.

She had learned a great deal about him and none of it had changed her feeling that his responsibilities were very much like those of her father, though on a much smaller scale. Everyone in the community seemed to like him. This was confirmed when the children were picked up and she received knowing grins and nods from Stella Kramer and Carol Saunders, which she took as a stamp of approval.

She couldn't wait to see Jace that night and drifted through her preparations for the next day in a happy bubble which was punctured when she returned to her little house after school to find she had a message waiting from Esther. She didn't take her cell phone to school because it might be distracting if her father called. He didn't like leaving messages and would keep calling until she answered. Instead, she depended on the phone Jace had given her for school-related calls.

When she dialed Esther, she was answered by her breathless lady-in-waiting who blurted, "Where have you been? I tried to call you after that pitiful meal they called breakfast, then after our morning torture race through the desert, then again after my five-celery-stick lunch! You could at least answer your phone."

"I was teaching, Esther, you know that," Alexis answered, flopping down on her seat sprung old sofa and chuckling at Esther's aggrieved tone. "What was so important, anyway?"

"I spotted some of those wicked reporters outside the spa. They were talking to some of the grounds-keepers."

Dread settled in Alexis's stomach. "How did you know that's who they were? Maybe they were tourists asking directions."

"Your Highness, this place is at the end of a private road. No one comes here simply to ask directions. Besides, one of them was someone I recognized—a man who Bevins had thrown out of that reception last year for the Spanish ambassador. He had a tiny camera hidden in his palm and was snapping pictures of all the guests. You remember him, bald, and has a face like a ferret."

Alarmed, Alexis's mind formed an instant picture of Dag Skold, a particularly aggressive and sneaky member of the paparazzi. "Did he see you?"

"I'm afraid so," Esther moaned. "I was behind the others as we returned from the morning nature trek through the cactus. One of the groundskeepers pointed at me with one hand while he slipped some cash into his pocket with the other. I think he must be new, hasn't learned he can be fired for that kind of thing.''

Alexis rolled her eyes at Esther's way of getting sidetracked. "What did you do, Esther?''

"I jumped behind a saguaro cactus, but,'' she sighed gustily, "I'm wider than it is and I kind of stuck out on each side.''

"And that's what they photographed?'' In spite of her worry, Alexis smiled at the image.

"Yes. Then I pulled my hat down over my face and dashed inside the wall—did you know this whole place is walled so we can't escape?'' she added in outrage. "It's like a plush prison.''

Before Esther could get started on that topic, Alexis interrupted. "Do you think you fooled them?''

"I don't know. You and I look a little bit alike, but I outweigh you by about fifty pounds—well forty now.'' A silence stretched between the two women as they thought about the possible consequences of this.

"Alexis,'' Esther said hesitantly, dropping the more formal means of address she sometimes used. "I don't think we're going to be able to carry this off much longer.''

"Don't say that,'' she commanded abruptly. "I've started making real progress this week. We're having an open house this Friday night. All the parents are invited. There's going to be a barbecue, and…'' Her voice died away.

Alexis didn't even want to think of the possibility of leaving after only a few weeks. She loved it here, loved working with the students, teaching them and assessing their progress, becoming part of the community. More urgently, she didn't want to leave Jace.

She had finished the business of thinking she was falling in love with him. She'd already fallen.

This realization sent a chill over her and she sat, staring at the blank wall opposite her as this truth slowly sank in. Vaguely, she could hear Esther babbling away in her ear, but she wasn't listening.

Her love for Jace was the main reason among many that she didn't want to leave Sleepy River. She had never been in love before. The idea thrilled and terrified her, but to be in love with a man like Jace—strong, so sure of himself—somehow that was even more frightening.

"...think we should do?" Esther was asking. "If those pictures are published, His Highness Prince Michael is sure to see them and then the fat will really be in the fire—not that I have much fat left to go into a fire," she added.

"What?" Finally, Alexis attended to what her lady-in-waiting was saying.

"What should we do?" Esther repeated patiently.

"I'm not sure except to lie low. Stay out of sight."

Esther hitched in her breath as if someone had just popped her between the shoulder blades. "I could pretend to be sick! Why didn't I think of that before?" Excitement rang in her voice. "I could stay in bed and have them bring me food. You know that old saying, 'Feed a cold and starve a fever'? I could pretend to have a cold." Esther was off, prattling happily about the possibility of staying in bed and being waited on rather than stomping about on hikes or sweating her way through aerobics classes.

Meanwhile, Alexis worried. She was very much afraid that Esther was right. They couldn't carry on this charade much longer. Deeply dismayed, she told her friend to handle it however she saw fit. She hung up with sick disappointment choking her.

She didn't want to leave, to abandon what she had begun, but she was very much afraid that's what she would have to do.

Slowly, she stood up and moved toward her bedroom. Jace was coming in an hour or so and she planned to prepare one of the few dishes she could cook expertly, herb-baked chicken and potatoes.

Nervously, she ran her palms down her thighs as she considered whether or not to tell him what Esther had said. She decided not to. It was unlikely that the paparazzi would be able to find her here. If Esther did as she planned and went to bed with a ''cold,'' the reporters would probably lose interest and go off to stalk someone else. Relieved and cheered by that thought, Alexis hurried to change clothes.

Alexis's relief lasted until about five minutes before Jace arrived when she received another phone call, this one from her father.

''Alexis,'' Prince Michael said, in ringing tones. ''I think you've been at that place long enough. There are no further improvements that you need to make to yourself in order to attract a husband. You realize, of course, that it's not only your looks, but your title and connections that appeal to the men I've found for you to choose from.''

Alexis winced. Royal, he might be. Tactful, he was not. ''Thanks a lot, Dad,'' she responded dryly. ''You sure know how to make a princess feel wanted.''

''Well, hmm,'' he blustered. ''You know what I mean.''

''Dad, why don't you think I can find my own husband if I should ever choose to have one?'' she asked in exasperation.

''I've been watching your sisters for several years now, that's why. Besides, I've seen this happen in other families, too. Why, the Marquis of Sunderland barely found out in time that the man his daughter was about to marry was deeply in debt and already had a mistress on the side.''

''Well, I'll be sure to avoid him, whoever he is, but I can certainly find my own husband.''

''That's why you're hiding out in Arizona, isn't it?'' Prince Michael demanded. ''You don't want me interfering in your life. I hear the same thing from Anya and Deirdre.''

''But do you listen?''

''You're my daughters,'' he reminded her in his thundering tones. ''I'm supposed to look out for you.''

''Yes, but not smother us,'' Alexis answered. This was an old argument which she doubted she would win.

He ignored that. ''It's time for you to come home. You have duties here.''

She glanced out the window to see Jace arriving in

his truck. A sudden feeling of panic swept over her. She didn't want to hurt her father, but she couldn't go home yet. For the first time ever, she was having a taste of real freedom, of being needed.

Jace stepped down from his truck, slammed the door and strode toward the teacherage, his long legs covering the ground in swift strides. He took off his cowboy hat and she could see his mahogany brown hair shining with red highlights as he was backlit by the setting sun.

Wanted. She was also having a taste of being wanted by Jace McTaggart. It was wonderful, heady stuff, and she didn't want to give it up. He didn't love her as she loved him, but he liked her and he wanted to be with her. In fact, he'd wanted that before he had known who she really was. He hadn't been interested in her title, connections, or money. Staying here with him and the people who knew her only as Alexis Chastain was more important to her than going back to Inbourg or doing what her father wanted. And yet she was torn and dismayed by the thought of upsetting her father. She loved him in spite of his controlling ways and she had never doubted that he loved her and her sisters and Jean Louis.

"Dad," she said desperately as Jace's knock sounded on the door. "I've got other obligations, too. Obligations to myself and...to other people."

"More important than your obligations to the people of Inbourg?" he asked, outraged. "I don't think so."

Confused and heartsick, she said, "I've got to go, Dad. I've got...someone here."

"Who?" he squawked. "A man? I want to know what's going on. Something doesn't sound right about that Golden Bluff Spa. Let me talk to Esther. I thought she was supposed to be chaperoning you."

"Goodbye, Dad," Alexis responded gently. "I love you and I'll talk to you in a few days." She quickly broke the connection, turned the phone off so it wouldn't ring again, and put it down before answering Jace's knock.

She opened the door and stared hungrily into his face. "Hello," she said.

He stepped inside and his dark eyes swept over her distraught face. Automatically, his arms went around her. She was glad to put hers around his waist and lean into him.

"What's the matter, Alexis?" His deep voice rumbled in his chest and his breath brushed the top of her hair.

"The world is rushing in on me," she said shakily, then pulled away slightly and looked into his face, her gaze tracing the concern she saw there even as she admired the strength and resolve that accompanied it. "Do you ever feel like that?"

"Sometimes," he answered slowly. "But I doubt that I feel it as much as you do because my world pretty much consists of my ranch and this community."

While yours is a much larger world. He didn't say it, but Alexis thought that was probably what he meant and it underlined the differences between them, ones she didn't want to examine right now. Instead, she formed a smile and asked, "Are you hungry?"

He stared at her for a second as if he was considering whether or not to let her get away with changing the subject, then he gave a small chuckle and leaned over to kiss her lightly. "Starved," he growled.

With a shiver of delight, Alexis wrapped her arms around his neck and kissed him back.

By Friday night, Alexis had almost forgotten her fears. The children had been so excited about the open house to which their parents were invited, and the barbecue that was to be part of the evening, that it had taken all of her disciplinary skills to keep them focused. She'd had little time to think about tabloid reporters or her father, or anything else. She had called Esther, though, who had reported her ploy seemed to be working. She had faked a cold, was happily entrenched in her bed at the spa, and the reporters seemed to have lost interest.

Now Alexis looked happily around the school yard. All the parents and children had come, as well as the school board members, and she wondered how many of her colleagues could boast a one hundred percent turnout for an open house. Even Luke Braden had come, though his nephew had not yet arrived.

A baseball game was going on in the gathering twilight and people were setting food out on long tables that had been set up on the lawn in front of the school. A couple of portable barbecue grills had been brought in and were being manned by Gil and Rocky, who seemed to feel that since they had mastered salad and salad dressing, they were ready for the big time.

Alexis was relieved that the two boys seemed to

accept her relationship with Jace, though Gil had pulled her aside to say soulfully, "I guess you know what you're doing, but if things don't work out, I'm available." Five minutes later, Rocky had told her the same thing. Fortunately, they'd been called to their duties at the grill before the suspicious looks they'd been exchanging could turn to blows.

When it got too dark to play baseball, everyone came in from the field, hot, sweaty and dusty, ready for food and drinks. Even Billy Saunders's dog, who had followed the family to the open house, had joined in the game and was now trotting beside his master with his tongue hanging and his sides heaving.

Alexis smiled as Billy found a plastic bowl and poured out water for his dog, then began telling everyone within earshot that Miss Chastain had told him that he was going to be allowed to build a snake house for the school and be the official school herpetologist. Martha Singleton had agreed to it, as well.

Billy's mother, Carol, approached Alexis with a grateful smile, "You have my undying gratitude for letting him do this. I know it sounds like a female stereotype, but I can't stand snakes. I'm glad he can have them at school. I'd offer you my firstborn son as payment, but, unfortunately, that's Billy," she said with a twinkle in her eyes.

Alexis started to answer, but Billy's dog suddenly stopped slurping his water, turned his head sharply, then went bawling and barking into the woods that edged the baseball field. Within seconds there was a yelp and a shout, and all the men sprinted in that direction.

"Has he bitten someone?" Alexis asked.

Carol started off. "I can't believe he has. He's never bitten anyone before, but he doesn't like strangers."

"Why would a stranger be around here?" Alexis asked, and then froze, dread forming a knot in her stomach.

Jace was the first to reach the woods. Loud crashing and thrashing sounded as the other men followed.

It was only seconds before Jace came out, pulling a struggling figure with him, a man who swung and shouted and tried to get away. When they reached the lights of the yard, Alexis was horrified to see the homely face and bald head of Dag Skold.

Chapter Ten

"If you don't want a lawsuit, cowboy, you'd better let go of me," the intruder shouted.

"If you don't want a broken jaw, you'll shut your mouth," Jace shot back. With one hand, he had a firm grip on the man's arm, and in the other hand, he carried a camera with the longest lens Jace had ever seen. He didn't know which one he'd rather crush—the man's windpipe, or his camera. The identity of this snake was still a mystery, but he had a pretty good idea why he was here. So did Alexis, he realized, when he glanced ahead to see her ashen face. His gut clenched at her look of dismay and at the way her bruised eye stood out against her pale skin.

When the photographer tried to pull away, Luke Braden appeared and wrapped his fist around the man's other arm. Between them, the two ranchers frog-marched him to the circle of light in front of the school and the small crowd gathered there.

"Who is this guy?" Stella Kramer asked, stepping forward. She spotted his camera and glanced nervously back at her daughters, then exchanged horrified looks with her husband, Dave. "Is he some kind of pervert?"

"You could say that," Jace answered grimly.

"Hey," the other man shouted. "I'm exercising my Constitutional rights. In case you didn't know it up here in the sticks, there's such a thing as freedom of the press."

"In case you didn't know it, there's such a thing as trying to walk on two broken legs," Jace responded. He looked across the shorter man's head at Luke, who nodded as if to say, "You take one, and I'll take the other."

"You wouldn't dare!" the reporter squeaked, his eyes bugging out and his throat clenching wildly.

Several people crowded around. "Jace, what's this all about?" someone asked.

Before he could answer, though, the man said, "I'm only here to photograph the princess. Papers will pay a lot of money for pictures of her living here in the boonies." His laugh was nasty as his gaze sought out Alexis, who was now looking positively sick. "Teaching school, are you, Your Highness? How quaint."

"Princess?" Stella echoed. "Is this guy nuts?"

"Your Highness?" Hattie Fritz had elbowed her way to stand before the man. "You think we're royalty here?"

Jace glanced across at Alexis who now looked like someone who had tried to escape a trap only to be caught in it again. He wanted to grab her, to protect her, give her back the radiant look she'd worn all evening. Things were spoiled for her now, and for him.

She looked up and met his eyes. She straightened, her chin lifted and her jaw hardened. He felt a surge of pride in her, followed by protectiveness. Damn, he wished he could have hustled the guy away, but she looked ready to face him.

"*I* am," Alexis said in calm, even tones. "I am Alexis Mary Charlotte of the house of Chastain and the principality of Inbourg."

Her announcement was met with deafening silence. As the Sleepy River residents exchanged stunned glances, she went on.

"This man is Dag Skold, a member of the paparazzi, a Dutchman, I believe, who spends his time stalking my sisters and me, sticking his nose in our business and generally making a nuisance of himself."

"The public has a right to know what you're doing," Skold bluffed, then winced as Jace and Luke simultaneously tightened their grip on his arms.

"No, they don't," Jace growled. "This is private property and you're a trespasser." He nodded at Luke, who swung the man around.

"I'll just see you to your car and out of these mountains," Luke said, as he hauled the man away. "I'll follow you in my truck to make sure you find your way. Lucky for you, I've got a rifle on the rack right behind the seat in case any dangerous animals come out of the woods.''

Skold gulped, his face whitening, but he managed to squawk, ''I want my camera.''

''Oh sure,'' Jace answered, opening the back, pulling out the film, and handing it over. ''Now get out.''

As Luke pulled Skold away, he shouted back over his shoulder. ''You think I'm the only one who knows you're a certified teacher? You think someone else won't think to check with the state to find out where you're teaching? Cute story, 'Princess Finds Out What The Simple Folk...' Ah!'' He yelped in pain as Luke demonstrated his rodeo-winning technique of throwing calves down to tie their feet together. A second later, he jerked the photographer out of the dust and hauled him away.

When they were gone, Jace turned to look around the circle of his friends and neighbors. All eyes were on Alexis, who was looking at him with distress in her eyes. He stepped to her side and put his arm around her shoulders, drawing her close to him. She trembled and then went still.

''Jace?'' Carol Saunders said. ''Did you know about this?''

''Yes,'' he admitted, glancing down at the top of Alexis's head where it rested trustingly against his shoulder. His arm tightened around her, and hers stole up to clasp his waist. ''But I didn't think she'd be pursued up here.''

''I'm sorry,'' Alexis said, her voice low and shaky as she looked from one person to another. ''I did everything I could to throw them off. I've always wanted to teach, but when you're in the public eye, it's hard. When I was doing my student teaching in Phoenix, the paparazzi hung around the school yard all the time, frightening the children...."

"And you thought our children wouldn't be frightened?" one mother asked, annoyed.

Alexis held out her hands beseechingly. "No, of course not, that's why I tried to hide my true identity. I registered at a health spa and sent my lady-in-waiting there in my place to throw them off, but..." Her voice faltered. "I'm sorry to say it didn't work. Dag Skold found me anyway. I'm so sorry."

A long silence followed as parents tried to decide what to say. A low muttering started and Jace tightened his arm around her. He knew he could intervene, tell everyone they had nothing to worry about, even though he wasn't quite sure that was true.

As head of the school board, he could talk to the other two members and convince them that since they had signed a contract with her, they couldn't ask her to leave. It could be a legal nightmare.

Jace looked around at the faces of his friends, then at Alexis, whose eyes were full of worry. The thought of her leaving had panic pummeling him in the gut.

God forbid that it should come to that.

What were they going to say? Alexis wouldn't blame the people of Sleepy River if they asked her to go. She hadn't been completely honest with anyone except Jace and even though she'd had the best intentions, it might not look that way to them.

"Miss Chastain?" Becky Kramer was tugging at her sleeve.

Absently, Alexis looked down to see a puzzled expression on the little girl's face.

"Are you really a princess?" she breathed. Her eyes were huge.

"Yes, I am." Alexis reached out to touch Becky's soft, red curls.

"Have you got a crown?"

"Oh yes."

Becky's eyes almost swallowed her face. "What's it look like?"

"It's gold and platinum with diamonds and rubies on it."

All the other little girls had joined Becky and were listening, goggle-eyed to this description. "Diamonds and rubies," they breathed, each of them, no doubt, imagining it on her own head.

"Can we see it?" one of the girls asked.

"Can we try it on?" another wanted to know.

Alexis laughed. "I'm sorry. It's not here. It's at my father's palace, locked away in a very strong vault in the dungeon."

"Palace," they gulped, looking at each other. "Dungeon."

They were staring at her with such awe, she knew they were no longer seeing her as the person who had taught them for two weeks, but as an exotic stranger who had landed in their midst. This dismayed her, but if the parents asked her to leave, anyway, out of fear for their children's privacy, it wouldn't matter how glamorous and exotic she appeared.

The one thing that she clung to, both physically and emotionally, was Jace's support. His arm held her tightly, and she was grateful to lean on his strength.

"So this kind of thing happens a lot?" Carol Saunders asked, breaking into Alexis's thoughts.

"Enough," she admitted. "Enough to make my family very cautious about what we do and where we go…and whom we involve in our lives."

"How do you avoid them?" another parent asked.

"Trickery," she said with a shrug. "Sometimes it works. Sometimes it doesn't."

"This time it didn't," Jace said.

"But this is a close-knit community," Hattie said, stepping forward. For tonight's party, she had added a flowered blouse to her usual outfit of a man's overalls and hat. She looked both festive and ready for anything. She gave Alexis a fierce look. "If any strangers come around, we'd know."

Alexis blinked. "What?"

"Yeah, we'd find 'em," Billy added. "Even Champ knew that guy wasn't supposed to be there." He bent down and gave his dog an affectionate scratch behind the ears. "I bet Champ could have run him off all by himself if Jace hadn't grabbed him instead."

"Yes, he's definitely a one-dog bodyguard squad," Jace said dryly.

"You're not thinking of leaving, are you?" Hattie asked. She turned to the people standing behind her. "You're not thinking of *asking* her to leave, are you? We still need a teacher around here and Martha can't take over again yet."

There was a general murmur among the adults, but the kids turned to them, begging to have Miss Chastain stay. Alexis thought it was funny that whereas the little girls had liked her before, as little girls usually like their teachers, now they adored her.

She took her arm from around Jace's waist and stepped away from the comfort of his arm. Lifting her hands, she called for quiet. "I don't want to put anyone at risk," she began.

"But they're not after any of us," someone said. "They're after you."

"It will still be a distraction to me and to the children if other reporters besides Dag Skold find me. Even though Luke has escorted him out of the mountains, he'll probably be back. He's not easy to stop, believe me."

"Why don't we members of the school board decide what to do?" Stella finally said, then her smile flickered. "Though I hardly think Jace is likely to be impartial."

Alexis felt a blush staining her cheeks, but fortunately, it was too dark to be seen. Jace drawled, "Nope, I probably won't be, but let's go inside and talk about it."

The three members started inside the building and Jace gave a gentle squeeze to Alexis's shoulder as he passed. When they were gone, the others returned to what they had been doing. The kids were persuaded by their parents to leave her alone and take up a game of flashlight tag.

Gil and Rocky went back to their barbecue grill and Alexis turned to them in surprise, realizing that they'd been uncharacteristically silent throughout the discussion. She found them looking at her as if she was a space alien who had just landed her flying saucer on the pitcher's mound.

She walked over to them. "Are you two all right?"

Gil's Adam's apple bounced ferociously a few times before he could form words. "We...we, uh, were surprised you decided you liked Jace better than one of us," he said. "Him being so old and all."

Alexis blinked. "He's thirty-one."

"Yeah, well, whatever. But why would a princess want him?"

"Yeah," Rocky broke in. "Do you princesses have some kind of cowboy fetish going on? 'Cause if you do, we were wondering if maybe your sisters would like us?"

Alexis barely gulped down an unladylike snort of laughter. What on earth went on in the brains of these two boys? She had to swallow quickly and clear her throat before she could respond. "Um, that's so...nice of you both, but actually my sisters both seem to be involved with other men just now, and besides, my oldest sister, Anya is almost Jace's age, probably too old for you, and..."

"Oh, that's okay," Gil said hastily. "We like older women. That's why we liked you right away. Experience and all."

"Gil," Jace's voice growled from above Alexis's head. "You left your single working brain cell at home. Maybe you'd better go get it."

Gil looked at his brother quizzically, then at Jace and Alexis. "Oh, uh, sorry. Said something I

shouldn't have, huh? Maybe I'd better stick to bar-
becuing?''

"Good idea," Jace responded, taking Alexis's arm
and drawing her away. Without preamble, he turned
her to face him and said, "We want you to stay."

Joy shot through her. "Oh, that's wonderful. Are
you sure, though? I don't want…"

"It was unanimous. We'll be damned if some
sleazebag is going to interrupt our lives. Anybody
comes around, we'll get rid of them."

Alexis laughed with joy and started to throw her
arms around him before recalling where she was and
landing back on her heels. If there'd been fewer people around, she would have kissed him.

He grinned and winked at her. "Later," he said.
With his arm around her, he drew her into the circle
of people, his friends and neighbors who were willing
to let her stay.

Alexis's happiness carried her through the next few
days, but on Tuesday something happened that pulled
the rug out from under her.

The children were at recess and Alexis was on the
playground with them, turning one end of a jump rope
when two of the older girls, who had gone to the
bathroom, darted back outside, shrieking, "Miss
Chastain, there's a man in the bathroom!"

Alarmed, she sent two of the older boys inside to
call Jace. Automatically, she ordered the other children to stay together while she hurried to find out who
the intruder was. On the way, she snatched up a base-

ball bat and entered the bathroom with a yell only to have flashbulbs explode in her face.

"Stop it!" she yelled, nearly blinded. "You're on private property. Get out right now!" All through this, the whir and click of the camera continued as a tall, overweight man with multiple cameras slung around his neck snapped one shot after another.

"Get out," she said again.

"Who you gonna call?" he sneered. "No body-guards here, Your Highness. Not even any cops."

She lifted the baseball bat only to have him grin and start clicking again, but when she banged it against a stall door, he seemed to realize she was serious.

"Hey, wait a minute," he said, stumbling back-ward as she banged the bat again. "You're not gonna hit me with that."

She was so angry, she thought she probably could hit a home run with his head, but she heard the thundering of hooves outside and pushed the door open to see Jace galloping up. He was off of Hondo's back in one leap and had the man by the scruff of the neck and the seat of the pants before the photographer knew what hit him.

Jace marched him outside, right in front of the children who were huddled together where she had left them. Within a few moments, they heard the roar of a motor and saw a cloud of dust rising into the air as the man streaked from wherever he had hidden his car and headed out of Sleepy River.

A few seconds later, Jace returned, swinging an

exposed roll of film from his hand. His face was grim and set in stone.

"I don't think he'll be back," he said tightly, then he glanced at the ruined film. "I'm getting good at this."

Tears spurted into Alexis's eyes. "But you shouldn't have to be good at it. And if that guy doesn't come back, someone else will," she choked. "Jace, this isn't going to work."

He stopped and his dark eyes swung to examine her distraught face. After one swift look, he turned to the children. "Everything's all right, but recess is over. You older kids, take the little ones inside so I can talk to Miss Chastain alone."

The children were unnaturally subdued as they filed back inside.

When they were alone, Jace gave her a severe look. "What are you talking about?"

She thew her hands into the air. "That guy, who-ever he was, frightened two of the girls. He was in their bathroom—no doubt because its window faces the playground. These people...they're relentless, they never give up. They're...they're the terminators of the news industry. They don't give *up*, I tell you."

His face set, he stepped forward and grabbed her arms, giving her a slight shake. "Alexis, stop it. You're hysterical."

She stopped and her breath jerked in calming breaths. She lifted tear-filled eyes to him. "I thought it would work, Jace. I really did. But I'm putting everyone at risk...."

"No."

"Yes. I had to call on you, interrupt your work to get rid of him."

"I don't mind," he said, but he was frowning at her fiercely.

"But how many more times will it happen?" she asked. She'd gone cold inside because she knew what she had to do, but she could barely stand to do it. She had begun to shake deep inside. In a few minutes, it would spread to the outside and she would be trembling like the leaves on the aspens that surrounded the playground. "And how many more times will the children be terrified of a stranger popping out of the bushes or accosting them in their own rest room?" Tears began to fall. "No. I've got to go." Her lips trembled as she went on. "I thought I could do this. I really did. I thought this was the place for me, but it isn't."

She saw anger flare in his eyes, but it seemed to be tinged with panic. "So you're going to just leave like this? What about your contract, your commitment?" He paused, his dark eyes searching her face. "What about us?"

Her laugh was hysterical. "I can't keep my commitment. I'm sorry. I'm putting the children at risk...." She broke off as an idea occurred to her. Hope sprang up as she looked at him. "You...you could come to Inbourg with me."

Stunned, he stared at her. "What?"

She clutched at him. "Come with me. We could live at the palace. The reporters have never made it into the palace, and..."

"I can't, Alexis, at least not for a few weeks. I've

got hay to finish getting in and the herd needs to be moved next week. I can't go off on a vacation."

"I didn't mean on a vacation. I meant permanently." She waited breathlessly for his response and when she saw sadness and regret flicker in his eyes, her heart sank.

"I can't," Jace repeated. He pulled her hands from his shirt and held them in his own. His rugged face was grim, set in lines that made him look years older.

Alexis shook her head as tears welled up and fell from her eyes. He was so solid, so real. She had come to depend on him as well as love him. She had wondered if he loved her and now she knew. She had all but fallen down on one knee and offered him a ring.

Her voice hitched as she answered. "No, of course you can't. You wouldn't want to live inside walls with bodyguards and alarm systems. It's a beautiful, beautiful palace, but in many ways, it's a prison. We can't even open the windows without setting off alarms."

"No, of course not," he said quickly, then checked himself. "I belong here."

"And I don't," she said quietly. "We both know that. We've been fooling ourselves." She saw his arms reaching for her in jerky motions as if they weren't sure what to do, but she turned away. "I've got to get back inside and talk to the children. Would you please call Martha and see if something can be worked out? Tell her…" Tears choked her. "Tell her how very sorry I am."

"Alexis, wait," Jace said, his voice gruff, but she hurried past him and into the schoolhouse to tell the children she was leaving. As she paused on the porch and tried to compose what she was going to say, she heard the thud of Hondo's hooves on the hard-packed earth of the baseball diamond, carrying Jace away, out of her life.

Chapter Eleven

"Coming home was the most sensible thing you could have done," Prince Michael said. Since Inbourg had no big international airport, Alexis and Esther had landed in Paris, then taken a smaller plane home. He had been there to meet them at the airstrip.

The three of them were walking together across the tarmac. In spite of the rush in which she had left Sleepy River, and the stressful journey home, she was glad to be back in Inbourg. She loved it, its people, and especially the handsome prince who ruled it.

She glanced up at her tall, regal father. He was slim and strong and now that the strain of rewriting the national constitution was over, years seemed to have dropped from him. Reaching up, she linked her arm with his and he patted her hand.

"I'm glad to be home, Dad. I can't wait to see everyone. What's been happening?"

He launched into a description of Deirdre's return to Inbourg with her new boyfriend, of Jean Louis's school days, but Alexis's mind drifted away, back to the mountains where she had known such peace.

Jace had come to say goodbye and help her load her car and lock the teacherage. It had been so painful for them both, he'd left after only a few minutes, driving away in his truck while she'd stood beside Rachel's little car with its smashed bumper and watched him go.

Alexis had driven the endless miles back to Phoenix, picked up a hugely grateful—and slimmed down—Esther at the spa, left Rachel's car at a garage to be repaired, and flown home. Jace had been in her thoughts every minute of that time.

She couldn't forget the way she had begged him to come with her and the way he had turned her down. She didn't know why she had asked, except that she loved him and wanted to be with him. Deep in her heart, she had known he wouldn't leave, though. He was right. He belonged at the Running M, and she didn't.

"...look fine," her father was saying. "I don't know what you were thinking, going back to Arizona, of all places. I would have thought you'd had enough of that place during your college years. Well, anyway, you're home now and that's what's important. Tomorrow night, there's a reception for an international company that wants to relocate to Inbourg. They've heard about the tax breaks we're offering as incentives. The man who runs the company is interested in meeting you."

Alexis finally focused in on what her father was saying. She leaned back and exchanged a look with Esther, who rolled her eyes humorously and mouthed the words, "Be tactful."

"Dad," Alexis broke in. "I'll be happy to attend the reception with you and meet the president of this company, but I won't be marrying him, or anyone else for that matter."

He stopped and gaped at her. His long, patrician nose fairly quivered. "What?"

Alexis took a deep breath. "Dad, I haven't been at the Golden Bluff Spa. Esther went in my place, that's why she looks so wonderful. I've been teaching school in a one-room schoolhouse in the mountains. I loved it. I loved everything about it, working with the children, living in the quiet of the mountains, but I couldn't stay because the paparazzi found me, disrupted the school, and made it impossible for me to stay. Teaching is my vocation, Dad. That's what I'm good at and it's what I want to pursue. I'm going to begin working on a project to improve the schools here in Inbourg. I hope I can count on your support, but I'll go ahead, even if you don't support me.

"Oh, and by the way," she finished, giving her father a loving smile. "I have no intention of marrying any of these men you've found, though if you need me to go to receptions and dinners I will if I have the time."

"Not...?" the prince sputtered. "Now see here, young lady, you've got the wrong idea if you think you can just flit home and start telling me what you're going to do. You're still a member of the House of Chastain, and..."

"Which I'm very proud to be," she broke in relentlessly. "But I didn't spend four years in college getting a degree in education simply to let it gather dust on a shelf while I swan around with the jet set looking for a husband." She took yet another deep breath because the next thing she was going to say was painful. "Dad, listen to me. I met someone in Arizona and fell in love with him. We can't be together because his life is there, and...and mine isn't, but I love him and I don't want anyone else."

Prince Michael was staring down at her in wonder. She gave him a sweet smile, squeezed his arm, then with a nod, Alexis moved ahead to where his car waited in the spot reserved for members of their family. It was an older Mercedes-Benz limousine his chauffeur had been driving him around in for as long as she could remember.

"Hello, Landis," she said to the stooped gentleman who held the door for her. "How's the family?"

Prince Michael followed, too stunned to say anything. Behind him, Esther walked, big-eyed and silent, but she gave Alexis a thumbs-up, signaling her support.

As she had expected he would, Prince Michael questioned her relentlessly on the drive to the palace. Alexis answered him with enthusiasm, describing the Sleepy River community, the school and the children. She refused to say anything more about Jace because it was still too raw, but he finally seemed to understand that she had plans and ideas which would improve educational standards in their country, though he wasn't sure if the entrenched old guard of the Ministry of Education would listen to her.

"Well, then," she told him as they pulled into the palace drive. "I'll simply have to change their minds."

She was delighted to see her sisters and Jean Louis, who all enjoyed hearing about her adventures in Arizona. Anya was taking on more and more of their father's work and was busier than ever. Deirdre was running the charity she and Anya had founded as well as spending time with her new love, who was a wealthy horse breeder as Alexis had suspected. Jean Louis was happily leading a group of his school friends into scrapes.

Alexis's firm stand that she had work of her own to do convinced the family to let her go her own way. No one expected her to be responsible for Jean Louis unless she chose to do so.

The second day after she arrived home, she began her campaign to improve the schools in the principality.

It was as difficult as her father had predicted. Her ideas were condemned as unworkable, but Alexis went to the administrators of Jean Louis's school and asked for their help. She needed records of student performance in order to work up statistics to prove her point and they let her have them.

Prince Michael was so impressed by her single-minded dedication to the project that he convinced the state treasurer to release funds to hire consultants to help her. Within two weeks, she was directing a group of people with doctorates, which she found highly ironic since she had a bachelor's degree and all of three weeks' teaching experience.

Long hours were spent in meetings and conferences, hours in which she was grateful to have her mind occupied because then she wasn't thinking about Jace.

He hadn't contacted her, though she had called and left a message with Gil that she had arrived home safely. Being away from Jace hurt, but having him ignore her call hurt even more. By the time she had been home for two weeks and she had heard nothing from him, she realized with intense pain that he wasn't going to call her at all.

"Don't ever fall in love again, Alexis," she muttered to herself one day as she climbed the stairs to the long gallery where pictures of her ancestors were hung. Jean Louis and his friends had been allowed to play in the old nursery up here, but now she had to round them up and send the little boys home. "Falling in love hurts too much. Especially if it's to a stubborn cowboy who doesn't love you back."

As she passed through the long rows of pictures, she glanced up to see Hedrick the Henchman, her ancestor whose memory Jace had called up. She stopped and gazed into the painted brown eyes and arrogantly curled lips, and wondered why she'd ever thought Jace was like this cold image.

She pressed her hands against the sudden ache of emptiness in her stomach and her shoulders slumped. She missed him so much sometimes it was hard to breathe. As she turned away from the painting, she spotted a small tapestry and stood gazing at it for long moments. It had always been one of her favorites, a woodland scene with a small, rock house that reminded her of the Running M. It wasn't particularly old or valuable, but it was beautiful.

Impulsively, she reached up to take it off the wall. She would ask her father if she could send it to Jace to replace the quilt she'd ruined. Holding it in front of her, she turned and glimpsed someone at the far end of the gallery.

For an instant, she thought it was Jace, then blinked as she admonished herself to stop living in a fantasy world. But when the man began to move forward, walking with a long easy stride, Alexis knew it was him.

Instead of the jeans and boots she'd always seen him wear, he was dressed in a suit with a snowy white shirt and a dark red tie. He looked like a banker instead of a rancher, but it was Jace all right.

The room seemed to spin around her and she grabbed the back of a chair for support.

He was before her swiftly, putting his arms around her and saying, "Hey, is that any way to say hello?"

"Jace," she said, hardly able to believe what she was seeing. Her eyes were huge as she searched his face. "How did you get in here?"

"Some nice guy named Bevins made the guards let me in. He said Esther had told him all about me. Esther being your lady-in-waiting, right?"

She had stood stunned throughout this little speech, but now she nodded. "Yes, she's my..." She broke off to run her hands along his arms. He was really here. "But what are you doing here?"

He shrugged in the characteristic way of his. "Everyone in Sleepy River is mad at me, so I'm not sure they'll let me live there anymore." His eyes twinkled at her.

"What?" She reached up to touch his face. Realizing she was still holding the tapestry, she dropped it onto a nearby table.

"They couldn't believe I let you get away, so now they're mad at me, especially the kids. They won't even let me umpire their ball games anymore. Hattie Fritz threatened to set her bees loose on me if I didn't come get you."

Alexis looked up at him in some confusion. "You're here because you want to umpire ball games and you're afraid of bees?"

He laughed. "No, I'm here to accept your proposal."

"What?" She blinked. "My proposal?"

"Isn't that what you meant when you asked me to come with you?"

"I don't know...." Her face turned red. "I wanted you to be here. I didn't want to be away from you...."

"Sounds like marriage to me," he said matter-of-factly. "Don't tell me you're taking back your proposal."

"But how can we do this? There are still the same problems," she said, not allowing herself to hope.

He lifted his chin. "I forgot to mention one thing. I love you."

"Oh." All expression wiped from her face. She

didn't know what to think. "But you didn't return my call. I thought you didn't care that I was gone."

He grimaced. "I was a fool, mad that you hadn't stuck around to work things out."

"I didn't see a way." She gave a disbelieving laugh. "I still don't."

"We'll get to that in a minute. I think you forgot to mention that you love me, too, Alexis."

"You're right," she said.

Jace took her into his arms and kissed her. She melted against him, glad to have him back. "Now's as good a time as any," he said.

"I love you, Jace," she responded dutifully. "But now what?"

He pulled her over to a chair that stood beneath tall plate glass windows looking out over the beautifully sculptured palace grounds. He sat down and pulled her onto his lap. Happily, she looped her arms around his neck.

"I had a lot of time to think," he said. "Nothing like being ostracized by the whole community to give a man time to think." His tone was dry.

"Even Gil and Rocky?"

"Especially Gil and Rocky. If they couldn't have you for themselves, they were at least willing to let me have you. They didn't speak to me until I told them I was on my way here." He tilted his head. "Actually, it was nice not having to listen to them. They didn't start in again until I announced I was coming to get you and they told me that I'd better not screw this up."

She kissed him. "You're doing fine so far. What

was it you were thinking about all those lonely hours?''

"You, of course, and why we couldn't be together."

She frowned. "I don't think I like the direction this is heading."

"Just wait. I accepted your proposal, didn't I?" He paused for a minute, gathering his thoughts. "It finally dawned on me that I can't let my fate out of my own hands. I'm just not made like that. But I kept remembering that quote of your mother's about a person being lucky if they know their place in the world. I thought the Running M was the only place for me. I guess it was because of being jerked around between my parents for so long. But you'd never had your fate in your own hands until you came to Arizona to teach, and even then you had to resort to subterfuge."

She winced. "Not my proudest moment."

"But you did it because you had to prove yourself. I don't want you to have to do that again. You have the right to live your life the way you want to, but you also have your duties to your family and to your country."

"Yes."

"But I want to marry you and be with you."

"How can we? The same problems still exist. I've got responsibilities here. The paparazzi won't leave me alone...."

"I think they will eventually. The boring wife of a rancher isn't going to make very good copy. When you need to be here in Inbourg, I'll be with you. When I need to be at the Running M, you'll be with me." His eyes were deep and serious. "I love you, Alexis. We can work this out."

Tears were standing in her eyes as she kissed him, ran her hand along his rugged jaw and said, "Of course we can, but there's something you should know about marrying a princess royal of Inbourg."

The warmth in his eyes changed to wariness. "What? That I have to be called Prince Jace?" he asked, shuddering.

"No, but we have to get my father's approval, the national council's approval and be counseled by the head of the church."

"All that?" He looped his hand in her long chestnut hair and tilted her head back so that their lips were only millimeters away. "How long will that take?"

"A few months." She breathed in a big sigh, bringing in the essence of him. "So we'd better get started."

"In a minute," he said, drawing her close for another kiss.

* * * * *

#1 *New York Times* bestselling author

NORA ROBERTS

brings you more of the loyal and loving,
tempestuous and tantalizing Stanislaski family.

Coming in February 2001

The Stanislaski Sisters

Natasha and Rachel

Though raised in the Old World traditions of their
family, fiery Natasha Stanislaski and cool, classy
Rachel Stanislaski are ready for a *new* world of love....

And also available in February 2001 from
Silhouette Special Edition, the newest book in the
heartwarming Stanislaski saga

CONSIDERING KATE

Natasha and Spencer Kimball's daughter Kate turns her
back on old dreams and returns to her hometown, where
she finds the *man* of her dreams.

Available at your favorite retail outlet.

Where love comes alive™

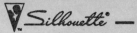

If you enjoyed what you just read,
then we've got an offer you can't resist!

Take 2 bestselling love stories FREE!

Plus get a FREE surprise gift!

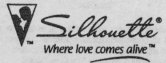

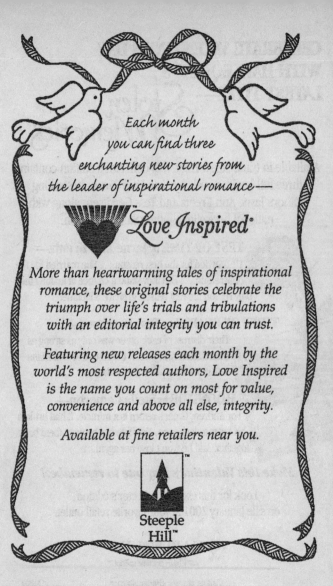

Each month
you can find three
enchanting new stories from
the leader of inspirational romance—

Love Inspired®

More than heartwarming tales of inspirational
romance, these original stories celebrate the
triumph over life's trials and tribulations
with an editorial integrity you can trust.

Featuring new releases each month by the
world's most respected authors, Love Inspired
is the name you count on most for value,
convenience and above all else, integrity.

Available at fine retailers near you.

Steeple
Hill™

CELEBRATE VALENTINE'S DAY WITH HARLEQUIN®'S LATEST TITLE— *Stolen Memories*

Available in trade-size format, this collector's edition contains three full-length novels by *New York Times* bestselling authors Jayne Ann Krentz and Tess Gerritsen, along with national bestselling author Stella Cameron.

TEST OF TIME by Jayne Ann Krentz—
He married for the best reason.... She married for the only reason.... Did they stand a chance at making the only reason the real reason to share a lifetime?

THIEF OF HEARTS by Tess Gerritsen—
Their distrust of each other was only as strong as their desire. And Jordan began to fear that Diana was more than just a thief of hearts.

MOONTIDE by Stella Cameron—
For Andrew, Greer's return is a miracle. It had broken his heart to let her go. Now fate has brought them back together. And he won't lose her again...

Make this Valentine's Day one to remember!

Look for this exciting collector's edition on sale January 2001 at your favorite retail outlet.

HARLEQUIN®
Makes any time special ™

Visit us at www.eHarlequin.com

PHSM